ROB JONES

THE
MIDNIGHT
SYNDICATE

JOE HAWKE #19

Copyright © 2024 by Rob Jones

All rights reserved. No part of this publication may be used, reproduced, distributed or transmitted in any form or by any means, electronic, mechanical, photocopying, recording or otherwise, without the prior written permission of the author or publisher, except in the case of brief quotations embodied in critical reviews and certain other non-commercial uses permitted by copyright law.

THE MIDNIGHT SYNDICATE is a work of fiction. All names, characters, places and occurrences are entirely fictional products of the author's imagination or are used fictitiously. Any resemblance to current events or locales, or to persons living or dead, is entirely coincidental.

This book is sold subject to the condition that it shall not, by way of trade or otherwise, be lent, re-sold, hired out or otherwise circulated in any form of binding or cover other than that in which it is published and without a similar condition including this condition being imposed on the subsequent purchaser.

ISBN: 9798332007507

Dedication

For My Family

CHAPTER ONE

"I could get used to this place," Lea said, lifting an iced Irish whiskey to her lips and taking a long, slow sip.

Hawke was rearranging the fire with a poker, pushing its tip into the glowing logs and sending a shower of fiery sparks up the chimney. "We deserve it after Scorpion Island."

"We deserve a sodding early retirement after Scorpion Island," Scarlet said.

Everyone laughed. Hawke set down the poker against the hearth's beautiful bespoke ironwork, walked back to the table they were sharing, sat back down and drank some of his whiskey. For what it was worth, he disagreed with Scarlet. He believed Scorpion Island was just part of the job, but a job he was starting to think twice about. He had fallen into ECHO almost by accident all those years ago, meeting up with Lea Donovan at the British Museum during a terror attack there. All that seemed like an impossibly long time ago. He had changed so much in the intervening years, and so had the world around him. Life had changed much since those early days; he could barely recognise it.

"We did good work on that island," he said. "Taking the Scorpion and his vile biological warfare programme out of the game was a job well done."

"I never said we didn't do good work," Scarlet said tartly. "I was making a joke."

Hawke stared at the English aristocrat, his old flame so many years ago. She was sitting opposite him, and gazing over her shoulder provided a stunning view of Telluride through their ski lodge window. Thick, rich swathes of snow piled up in smooth banks, as if carved out of frozen cream, leading the eye to a line of tall fir trees, their branches also caked white from the recent snowfall. Behind it all, the view was framed by the snow-capped ridge of the San Juan Mountains. Lit now by the neon-pink alpenglow outside, the lodge itself was a marvel of reclaimed hardwood and natural granite, all under a vaulted ceiling. It was a luxury chalet experience that came with a small staff to cater to their every need. No one wanted to go home.

"I know you were telling a joke," he said quietly, swilling his whiskey and looking down wistfully into the amber liquid in his tumbler. "Something I find harder and harder to do these days."

Lea reached out and put her arm around his shoulder. The atmosphere seemed to tighten. "It was pretty good of old Richard to lay this on for us," Alex said, warming things up. "Who knew he had it in him?"

"Who knew we had the budget?" Ryan asked.

Lea smiled. "Don't get used to it. Rich will want us back in Elysium sooner or later."

"Elysium? Maybe we should rename it Asylum!" Scarlet said. "I'm starting to go insane in that place."

"*Starting* to go insane?" Ryan said, sipping his beer. "Are you kidding me? You've been insane for years."

"That's what living in close proximity to you can do to a girl."

"Girl, eh?" Ryan said. "There's certainly nothing wrong with your optimism."

Scarlet reached for Ryan's beer, presumably to grab it and tip it over his head, but Ryan leapt up from his seat and stepped back a few paces, laughing as he went. "Ha!

Not this time, Cairo!" he said triumphantly. "Thank you all the same!"

Scarlet casually took her rum and coke and tipped a small pool of it all over the seat where Ryan had been sitting and then looked up at him with a big smile on her face. "You're more than welcome, boy."

Another wave of laughter, and then the smell of succulent beef and mustard drifted through to them from the kitchen. The chalet's small staff included a young local Coloradoan woman called Madison who was in charge of a catering team of one - her. No one had ever tasted food as good as hers before, and now she was busy cooking up some homemade burgers after their long day on the slopes.

"I'm not worried about going back," Alex said. "I like it on Elysium. I wonder what Ravi and Kahlia think?"

"They're sunning themselves in Rio right now," Scarlet said. "So they're probably too drunk to think."

"Considering Ravi grew up in one of the most violent and dangerous favelas in Rio de Janeiro, I'd say he loves Elysium just fine," Lea said.

After a short but peaceful lull in the conversation, Ryan spoke next. "I can't believe that we were standing on the beach on Scorpion Island watching that bloody volcano blow up just a couple of weeks ago. Talk about chalk and cheese."

"Time sure does fly when you're having fun," said Alex.

"I'm with Lea," Reaper said. "I could get used to this place, too. I'm older than most of you guys. I'm not gonna complain if I wake up in a luxury ski chalet and know the day ahead is going to be spent playing on the slopes and then coming home to a fine meal and a robust red. Call me old-fashioned but that's just the way it is."

After having lived with Lea for so many years, Hawke was in no doubt that she meant what she had just said. Lea was as strong and courageous and as loyal as they came, especially to Sir Richard Eden who had effectively acted as a surrogate father to her after her own father's premature demise. But like the rest of the team, Hawke knew she was not getting any younger and she had on occasion talked to him about how nice it would be to take a longer break in between missions. He was on the verge of asking her and everyone else at the table if they would like another drink from the bar to go with their evening meal when Lea's telephone rang.

She reached for the telephone from her denim jacket pocket, prompting everyone else at the table to share a surreptitious and vaguely anxious glance.

Hawke met Lea's eyes a second after she had read the caller ID. He recognised the look at once and knew it meant business. This was confirmed a second later when she told everyone at the table that the caller was Richard Eden, then she rose from the table, put the phone to her ear and walked over to one of the French doors leading out onto the balcony running around the west side of the chalet. She opened the door and stepped outside, leaving everyone at the table to stew for a few moments in nervous anticipation.

Scarlet ran her hand up Reaper's forearm, squeezing it. "What were you saying about getting used to this place?"

"I was looking forward to having a go at Senior's Run, too," Hawke said, referring to one of the most challenging ski runs in North America, up at Palmyra Peak.

"Looks like you can forget that," Alex said. "At least if the look on Lea's face is anything to go by."

Hawke turned and saw Lea walk back into the room, bringing a gust of icy wind with her. She was still holding her telephone but no longer talking to Eden. She walked straight over to the plasma television screen up on the wall high above the fireplace, picked up the remote and turned it on. Then she screen-mirrored her phone onto the plasma screen and turned to face the rest of the team. In the background, Madison made a clattering sound in the kitchen, reminding Lea to step over, speak to her for a moment and then close the door.

"Okay everyone," Lea said, "get your sorry arses over here and get comfortable. Rich wants to talk to us about a job and there's not a lot of time."

"When is there ever a lot of time?" Scarlet said, scoffing. "We seem to live on the very edge of time."

Hawke got up from the table and walked over to the collection of soft, comfortable chairs around the large fireplace in the main living area of the chalet. He crashed down on one of the single-seater leather recliners and took another long sip of the whiskey, his mind already going through all the various scenarios that were most likely to unfold in the next few moments. As he leaned back in the comfortable seat and regarded the image of Eden being projected from Lea's phone onto the large plasma screen on the wall, he knew it would be nothing good.

"Good evening everyone," Sir Richard Eden began.

Scarlet sighed. "Here it comes. Brace for impact."

"Why does something tell me you're about to ruin our vacation, Richard?" Alex asked.

Eden smiled, it was polite but not exactly full of emotion. "Earlier today, I had a very interesting conversation with a British government official regarding a man named Dr Tamu Haggblom. Those of you who are keeping up to date with the weaponization of artificial intelligence will no doubt be aware of him."

"Weaponization of artificial intelligence," Scarlet repeated softly. "Oh, joyful day."

"I've read about Haggblom," Alex said.

"Me too," Ryan said. "It was an article in the Journal of Machine Learning Research a few weeks back. In my opinion, he's a total genius. He's working right at the cutting-edge intersection of quantum computing, deep learning and neural networks. I mean, this guy is all over this stuff like a nasty rash."

"Yes, that's one way of putting it," Eden said. "But as Ryan correctly points out, Haggblom is an extremely accomplished man with a doctorate in computer science from the Massachusetts Institute of Technology, where he specialised in quantum computing and what was, at least back then, a very early form of artificial intelligence. He went on to do important work at the Cybernetic Intelligence Research Institute and after that, he dropped off the radar. Since then, I haven't heard from him and neither has anybody else. It doesn't take a genius to work out that he'd been picked up by a covert government organisation and found gainful employment in creating presumably Top Secret artificial intelligence weapons systems."

"What did this British government official want exactly, Rich?" Lea asked.

"As I had suspected, he confirmed Haggblom has been working on a Top Secret project for a joint British-American defence project, and he was understandably unwilling to share too many details with me, even though I have very high-security clearance. He got in touch with me because he's looking for a quiet, respectable and effective team to chaperone Professor Haggblom on a rare outing from his underground base somewhere in Wiltshire."

"Quiet, respectable and effective?" Scarlet said. "That counts us out then."

Alex gave her a look. "Where is Haggblom going exactly, Rich?"

"He is meeting with his American counterpart in New York City, and when I say a counterpart I mean the director of research for the American end of the project. Normally, they communicate via encrypted electronic signals, but they need to discuss something which requires them both to be in the same room. At this point, I have no further knowledge about what this is all about."

"You mean we're bloody babysitters?" Scarlet asked, downing her rum.

"No one's asking you to wipe clean any mouths or backsides, Cairo," Eden said. "You're simply being engaged to ensure Professor Haggblom can travel from Wiltshire to New York City and back again without incurring anything unpleasant."

"And no one else can do this?" she asked. "I'm just settling in here."

"No," Eden sighed. "You often tell me that you're the best of the best, Cairo. Do you recall that?"

Scarlet shrugged. "May have said it once or twice."

"Well, that's the thing about being the best of the best, isn't it?" Eden said. "You get asked to do jobs like this that no one else can do as well as you. Now stop whining, finish your drink, pack your bags and fly to England at the earliest possible convenience. When you land you will rendezvous with Professor Haggblom and his UK security team. Then it's over to you. And there's one more thing. It's not good."

"Shoot," Lea said.

Eden steepled his fingers. "Do you recall at the end of your mission on Scorpion Island telling me something that Scorpion had told you about an organisation called the Order of the Black Wolf?"

"Yes," Hawke said. "He told me personally that this Order of the Black Wolf was intending to steal the Poseidon's Trident from the Smithsonian."

"What's this got to do with Haggblom, Rich?" Lea asked.

"Probably nothing," Eden said grimly. "Because I recently intercepted a communiqué coming out of Greece from an arms broker dealing with the Order of the Black Wolf. I'm sorry to say I believe this organisation is headed up by Hugo Zaugg's daughter, Helga Zaugg."

Hawke's blood turned to ice. Lea went ashen. The rest of the team was stunned into total silence. Hugo Zaugg was the psychopath they had done battle with in their very first mission, only bringing his tyrannical rule to an end when Hawke had killed him with a sniper's rifle high in the Swiss Alps. Hawke had thought that when he sent Hugo Zaugg to the grave, that had ended the nightmare once and for all. Now he saw he was wrong.

"Not a good development," Reaper said.

Scarlet craned her neck to search the room for something. "I'll take more booze now."

They all heard Madison push through the kitchen door and appear in a cloud of steam. The room was immediately filled with the aroma of fresh home-cooking.

"Your burgers are ready!" Madison said, a silver tray in each hand and a beaming smile on her face. "And these guys are my best yet!"

"Any chance you could keep them warm for us?" Lea said.

Madison stopped and looked over at Lea, a little confused. "Sure, for how long?"

"A week all right?"

Hawke recognised the look on Madison's face. It was pretty much how he was feeling right now as well.

CHAPTER TWO

Kahlia Keahi was walking along Copacabana Beach with her feet in the warm sand, a smile on her face and the world-famous Sugarloaf Mountain directly ahead of her. She had come a long way from her gang warfare days back in Hawaii and while it was a journey she was proud to have made, she was glad now to be at what she hoped was the end of it. Joining the ECHO Team with Ravi was the best thing that had ever happened to her. She enjoyed the challenge, the work, the mutual trust and loyalty and most of all the feeling of being part of something more than a special operations unit, something more like a family.

Earlier, back on Avenue Atlantica, she had bought a large flat white coffee, and now she finished the last few sips before turning left, to the east, and walking back towards the main part of Copacabana. As she walked, she drew the usual stares of disbelief as people took in her almost full-body tattoos, even here in Rio which wasn't exactly a conservative city, but she was more than used to it. The truth was, sometimes she regretted what some euphemistically called 'body art' but what she saw now as the indelible branding on her skin showing membership of gangs which she now hated more than words could express. There was little she could do about it now. They were part of her just as much as anything in her psyche and she had learned to live with it.

She climbed onto her Vespa, kickstarted the engine, checked her mirrors and pulled away from the beach. It was a short cruise back to the apartment she and Ravi were sharing, having declined Sir Richard Eden's offer of taking a break in the Colorado Rockies. Ravi wanted to come to his hometown and meet up with old friends and family, and not only did she want to spend her time with her boyfriend, but she also was no fan of the cold and snow, having been born and brought up in Oahu.

Thinking of Sir Richard Eden on Elysium and the rest of the team in Telluride, her mind now drifted back to the many adventures she and Ravi had shared with Joe Hawke, Lea Donovan and the others. Never in her life had she encountered anyone like them. She shook her head in disbelief as she remembered conversations she'd had with

Alex Reeve, the daughter of a former American President, watched the devil-may-care Scarlet 'Cairo' Sloane do some of the most dangerous things she had ever seen in her life, or the long hours of conversation she'd spent, sometimes through the night, talking to the walking internet that was Ryan Bale. Their friendly faces drifted through her mind as she cruised south along Avenue Atlantica before turning right onto one of the city's most famous tree-lined boulevards, lined on either side with beautiful colonial-style buildings, before finally turning another right onto the Rua Santa Clara, where she and Ravi were renting their apartment at the foot of Cabritos Hill, the big brother of Sugarloaf Mountain, but located at the far south of Copacabana.

She pulled the Vespa up to the side of the road parking beneath the thick rich foliage of a Brazilian pepper tree, killed the engine and climbed off the moped. It was summer here in Brazil, and the air was thick, sweaty and humid, a thick blanket of low grey clouds hung over the city almost threatening to smother everyone in it, and she felt the sweat trickling down her back as she removed her helmet and crossed the pavement to her apartment building. She stared up at the 16-story-high tower block and considered taking a swim in the communal pool, up on the roof. She was home alone until at least lunchtime because Ravi had driven into Jacarezinho, a dangerous favela in the city's north zone, with over 60,000 residents, to meet up with some ghosts from his past. She had no fear for his safety because Ravi had grown up there and was more than capable of looking after himself.

She pushed open the lobby door and walked over to the lift where she selected the top floor and waited for it to arrive in the lobby. When it reached the ground floor, she stepped inside, selected her floor, and watched the doors brush gently closed. The lift jerked as it transported her up. At the top, the doors swept open and she stepped out into the corridor. She pulled her key from her pocket and opened her apartment door, directly opposite the lift.

Stepping inside her apartment, she closed the door behind her and made her way into the kitchen where she switched on the kettle and spooned some instant coffee into a mug. They never tasted great straight after a flat white bought from a shop, but she needed more caffeine.

She heard a door bang somewhere inside the apartment.

"Ravi?" She called out. "Did you already get back?"

Silence.

She felt her skin prickle with fear. She opened the top drawer where they kept the cutlery and pulled out a small serrated steak knife. Leaving the kettle boiling behind her, she stepped out of the kitchen and scanned the main living area for anything out of the ordinary. She saw nothing that worried her. The apartment was silent again. It sounded like the noise she had heard was the bedroom door on the other side of the living area. She had a choice now – she could step back outside the apartment, get in the lift, go down to the pavement and call Ravi, or she could go into the bedrooms and make sure the apartment was clear of danger.

It was a test she didn't intend to fail.

Kahlia was not exactly a shrinking violet. She had spent years in some of Hawaii's most dangerous gangs and spent the most recent years of her life in ECHO, fighting alongside former Special Forces operatives and Secret Service agents to defeat threats more disgusting than she could ever have imagined in her previous life. What was all of that for – what did all of that add up to – if she now turned tail and ran for the safety of her boyfriend?

She had made her decision and with the kettle rumbling behind her, she made her way across the living area and along the narrow, gloomy corridor that led to the bathroom and two bedrooms at the other end of the apartment. She saw a closed door ahead of her, the master bedroom door and her speculation that this was a door she had heard slam was now confirmed. The other two doors were ajar. Was it possible that a draught from an open window inside the bedroom had caused the door to close?

She doubted it. All of the windows in the apartment were closed.

She wondered what to do. Time seemed to slow. Everything went quiet.

Her skin prickled a second time.

She gripped the knife tighter.

That was when her bedroom door burst open and she was confronted with two tall, heavy-set figures dressed entirely in black, their faces hidden behind black balaclavas.

Her worst childhood nightmare had just come true.

CHAPTER THREE

Ravi Monteiro was a street fighter, so when they came for him on his home territory in the favela, he gave himself a better-than-fighting chance. But they'd startled him in the suddenness and ferociousness of their attack, putting him on the back foot. Just a few moments ago, he had been shooting the breeze with an old friend from way back when regaling him with his tales of the last few years of ECHO adventures. That had been fun, but the disadvantage was that he had sunk several beers with his old mate and was a little worse for wear. He had let his guard down.

But he had to have *some* time off the clock, right?

It wasn't feasible to be constantly expecting an attack and this was a well-deserved break after the horrors of Scorpion Island. He spent several good days relaxing and enjoying the Brazilian sunshine, getting to speak in his native Portuguese to his oldest friends and family, people who understood him the best, and tonight he was planning on taking Kahlia out for an expensive meal in Leblon, an upmarket part of the city.

Instead, he was now confronted by two large, hard-looking men dressed entirely in black combat fatigues, their faces obscured by black balaclavas. They looked like the kind of thing he was used to encountering on a mission somewhere strange and exotic with ECHO – perhaps Russian Spetsnaz, or a clandestine German Special Forces unit gone rogue – but here they looked completely incongruous, here on the dusty streets of the favela. This was a place where the threat came from young men dressed in old, greasy T-shirts and jeans, sometimes even wearing flip-flops. This was not a place where you usually saw commandos.

He was out in the street now, a few hundred yards from his friend's house and heading back out of the favela to get a cab. Some companies drove into the favela, but many preferred not to. Ravi was happy to walk a short distance to clear his mind of the booze before finding himself a ride home. But whoever was attacking him had waited until he was out of earshot of his friend's apartment. Perhaps they had tracked him along the filthy graffiti-covered back alleys of the favela and he had been too drunk to notice.

He cursed himself for being so shortsighted. Then he felt the hair stand up on the back of his neck as he thought of Kahlia. He had presumed she was safe back inside the apartment – or had she told him she was going for a run along the beach? Either way, he had presumed she was in no danger and had left her to drink with his old friend. He was now confronted not only with these two men but with the dreadful thought that perhaps others had also come for her.

The two-man team split apart. One moved around to his left while the other ran straight for him. Ravi was standing in a dog-leg alley and they were trying to pin him in and stop him from fleeing for his life. But did they mean to kill him? He had to presume so. And even with the beer flooding through his veins and muddying his mind, he knew he had to pull something out of the bag if he was to survive this attack. He could worry about who they were and why they had attacked him later.

The man in front of him now pulled a combat knife from a leather holster on his belt and continued his charge forward, while the man to his left was reaching out with both hands trying to kettle him in the corner of the dog leg. Ravi was well versed in several seriously lethal street fighting martial arts, not to mention all of the additional experience working with the ECHO team had given him, but he was now fighting against his mind to break through the wall of beer, which was slowing his response time and dumbing down his motor skills.

He stepped forward into the fight towards the first man and reached out to him, trying to disarm him and knock the knife to the ground. Thanks to the beer, he mistimed the move and the man was able to easily sidestep him before bringing the handle of the knife down on the back of his head. Ravi thought he was going to pass out and collapsed down to his knees. He was dimly aware of the other man who had kept him pinned down, now moving closer to him. He saw him in his peripheral vision as he also drew a knife from his belt. Ravi's head, already swimming in alcohol, was now swirling with the impact of the blow to the back of his head. He leaned forward and vomited wildly onto the ground as his vision slowly became tunnelled.

The two men stepped closer, each of them now brandishing a combat knife.

THE MIDNIGHT SYNDICATE

If he was going to live, Ravi had some thinking to do and not much time to do it.

CHAPTER FOUR

Kahlia tried hard not to be scared. She remembered her training, slowed her breathing, kept her heartbeat steady and assessed the situation with a calm and level head. Despite all this, her heart was telling her she stood no chance at all. Both of the men were gripping combat knives and moving towards her at a fast pace. There was no dithering. They knew what their target was and how to execute it with no delay. Between this and their clothes and weapons, she knew she was dealing with a highly professional outfit. These were no common hoodlums trying to rob her apartment after following her home from the beach.

She was still pumped from the coffee she'd had earlier on the beach and was grateful for the extra caffeine as her adrenaline kicked in giving her a double boost – heightened alertness and faster and more accurate motor skills. It would've been a different story if she had decided to open and drink the wine they had planned for later. The thought of this instantly brought Ravi into her mind. Her heart quickened. Her breath grew shorter. The men were approaching and she began to step backwards – a retreat physically and in her mind - from the threat before her.

She had been distracted by the thought of Ravi because she knew he was going to spend the afternoon drinking with his old friends in the favela. If these men who had come for her were on a mission to round them both up – did this have something to do with ECHO? – he would be easy to overcome. Ravi was the best street fighter she had ever seen, but when it was time to let his hair down he knew how to do it. Chances were, he was already fairly steaming by now and if this was some coordinated attack between the two of them, he would stand no chance at all. These terrible thoughts knocked her off a game, but she decided to fight on.

The truth was it wasn't her decision to fight on at all because now both of the men lunged at her and dragged her into the fight whether she liked it or not. The bigger man, the man now on her right who was slightly in front of the other man came at her with a vengeance, extending his arm as far as it would go and slashing at her face with the combat knife.

Kahlia flicked her head back to avoid a horrible scarring from the steel blade and simultaneously reached out and grabbed the man's arm as it sailed past her head, grabbing his wrist with her left hand and twisting it in the opposite direction. She heard a horrible snapping sound and the man screamed in pain and dropped the knife. Kahlia wasted none of the advantage she had seized, and as the other man now pushed past the first man and lunged towards her, she brought her elbow up into the first man's face and broke his nose. Then she turned and kneed him in the groin, ending the set course menu by bringing her right knee up and pulling his head down to meet it, smashing him unconscious and then pushing him backwards into the other man.

The second man was slimmer and faster than the first and easily managed to jump over his unconscious comrade before lunging towards her in a renewed attack. This man was also carrying a combat knife, but having learned from the mistake of his colleague, he decided to play a much closer hand, keeping the knife more as a defensive weapon than using it to slash her or stab her.

Keeping his arms close to his body to stop her from doing the same defensive move again, he moved towards her more cautiously, playing a different game. Without warning and moving much faster than the other man, he fired not his knife hand but his left hand into her face. It was the fastest punch she had ever seen, and his knuckles, concealed inside a black leather glove, made contact with her right temple and cracked the left side of her head into a picture hanging on the corridor wall behind her. It was a sharp hard blow and it smashed the glass out of the frame which now rained on the floor in lethal little shards, leaving her feeling nauseous and disoriented.

Her attacker did not rest on his laurels. Before she had fully recovered from the blow, he punched her a second time, this time in the centre of her face, just catching the side of her nose and colliding primarily with her cheekbone. If he had hit her directly in the centre of her nose she knew the blow would have smashed it to a pulp, but instead, the blow cracked her head back and drove it back into the wall for a second impact in the smashed glass hanging out of the frame. She fought hard not to give up.

The adrenaline was pumping through her like high-performance fuel. This was a fight or flight moment if ever there was one. She did not know who this man was or what he wanted with her but she had to presume he wanted her dead. If not now – for he would have finished the task with the knife if that was the case – then later perhaps in some depraved circumstances she did not even want to imagine. She lashed out in self-defence, kicking him in the shin and then driving her steak knife up towards his rib cage. She wasn't fast enough and the man easily swatted it out of her hand before driving his knife freehand up towards her throat and pinning her against the wall, restricting her breathing and pinning her in place.

She could see into his eyes now – dark brown eyes filled with a strange serene calmness she had not expected to see. She knew there was nothing she could do. She thought about bringing her knee up into the family jewels, but the man was too big and holding her at arm's length at this angle had placed that part of his body out of the reach of her knee. He began to nod his head and very quietly whispered to her in English that it was time for her to go to sleep now. At the same time, she felt his hand constricting around her throat and slowly, almost peacefully, she lost consciousness.

*

Ravi's world had shrunk down to a single square metre of favela sidewalk. He heard the men talking and realised when they used some carioca, some slang, they were locals.

Mina.

Porrada.

Mó B.O.

Ravi's mind whirled. Mina? Who was the girl? Porrada? Was *he* the challenge? Mó B.O? What was the serious situation? He wondered if he could make some kind of a bridge between them, knowing now that these were men local to this part of the city, but when he started to try and speak he got a hefty punch in the side of his head for his trouble which knocked him down fully onto the pavement. Before he could get up, one of the men kicked him full-force in the ribs with his riot boot and Ravi heard a desperate, horrifying crack before feeling a terrible pain radiating through his body. They had now nearly knocked him out twice and broken at least one of his ribs. There would be no bridge-building, only the plotting of revenge if he survived the attack.

He cursed his drunkenness one more time as he tried to stagger to his feet. Oddly, both the men let him make the journey and he soon found himself on his feet, swaying with the alcohol and the blows to his head like a drunken fool staring at the two assailants. Before he could consider his next move both men moved at once, slamming him up against the wall against and punching the air from his body. They doubled down on this manoeuvre with each man punching him in the stomach at the same time before the man on his left began firing a fusillade of blows into his face, one gloved fist after another and a never-ending blitz of punches.

Ravi was too drunk to change his fate and the last thing he saw was the man who had punched him in the face now drew his head back and fired a brutal headbutt right into the middle of his face. Then Ravi's world turned to black.

CHAPTER FIVE

It turned out that Joe Hawke had not missed London. He was leaning against the side of their hired SUV in the long-stay business car park just north of London Heathrow Airport's northern runway, collar up, wondering exactly how it was possible that it felt colder here than the snow-covered Rocky Mountains they had left a few short hours ago. Gunmetal grey clouds were scudding across the sky, so low they seemed almost to scrape the top of the control tower he was gazing at across the airfield. Icy drizzle brushed against his face at random intervals, and the dampness of the place seemed to penetrate his bones.

He turned his face to the sky. Every ninety seconds or so, another wide-body passenger jet broke through the clouds and screeched to a halt on the runway, coming in at the moment mainly from the east – Japan, Singapore, and India. He had flown in and out of this place more times than he could remember.

Hawke felt the car rock and then a door opened. It was Lea. She stepped out into the cold and closed the door gently behind her until it clicked. Her face was flushed from sitting in front of the heating vent for the last half hour.

"Haggblom is five minutes out," she said. "Just got a call from Rich."

"And do we finally get to know what car to look for?"

"He's being driven in a silver Volvo."

She read out the Volvo's number plate from memory.

Hawke scanned the car park's entrance for signs of the car, but nothing yet. It was immature and ungrateful, but he felt slightly annoyed at having been dragged away from their rest and relaxation break in Colorado to be engaged in what was for them at least a low-key and low-risk mission. In days so recent he could almost reach out and touch them, he had raced to save the United States from nuclear Armageddon, lost Lexi Zhang deep in the Congo, fighting the warlord King Kashala and his psychopathic mercenaries, and was almost killed along with several other members of his team on a private island belonging to a Yakuza chief named The Scorpion. Chatting with a mild-mannered professor on a private jet cruising across the Atlantic en route to a confidential conference for twenty-four hours and returning him safely home again seemed like a cakewalk in comparison.

But as they had discussed back in the ski chalet, maybe that wasn't such a bad thing. They needed time to take a break and recharge their batteries, to let their wounds heal, but as they all knew only too well, the physical wounds healed far quicker than the psychological ones. Lea had told him that was one of the reasons Richard Eden had sent them up to the Rockies to take a break rather than simply spend the downtime on Elysium – because there were too many things on the island that reminded them all of Lexi and their other fallen comrades.

Hawke respected Eden for that kind of thinking. Over his long military career in the Royal Marines Commandos and the Special Boat Service, Hawke had served with more good senior officers than he had suffered bad ones, but thankfully Eden was steadfastly in the former group. When people on the team were close to the edge or about to snap, he took appropriate action without dithering. He always protected his troops and ensured their well-being as far as he could.

Hawke's thoughts were ended abruptly by an elbow nudging his ribs.

"This is him," Lea was saying.

He looked across the SUV's wet roof and tracked a metallic silver Volvo XC40 as it turned into the car park. It drove around the perimeter of the car park, its inhabitants scanning for any sign of danger, before finally steering into their lane and pulling to a stop one space away. Inside, Hawke recognised at once the unmistakable figures of two close-protection security guards. One was driving and one was in the back with a man in his sixties.

Haggblom.

"The Eagle has landed, I guess," Lea said.

Hawke pushed away from the car and stepped towards the Volvo. "Then let's get that eagle out of here. We have a flight waiting."

CHAPTER SIX

"So, tell me Professor Haggblom," Lea asked. "Now we're safely cruising over Ireland on our way to New York City, perhaps you could give us a bit more information about what it is exactly you're researching for the government?"

Haggblom looked awkward, his eyes flitting from one member of the team to the other as he thought of a way out of Lea's question. That was her interpretation of his body language, at least. He shifted in his seat uncomfortably and then settled down to reply.

"I'm afraid I'm not at liberty to discuss the matter with you, Agent Donovan."

Lea gave him her best smile. She had already been briefed by Eden about Haggblom's almost certain reluctance to answer any further questions, but she felt that her part was responsible to at least inquire why they were engaging in the mission. She was doubtful that anything too dangerous was likely to occur, but as a team leader working directly under Eden's authority, she felt she could push the matter a little, for her curiosity if nothing else.

"I think we deserve to know a little more than that, Professor. Any one of us could take a bullet for you in the next twenty-four hours, after all. Or worse."

Haggblom shifted in his seat again and his beady eyes once again flitted from one member of the team to the other, lingering for a little longer perhaps on Hawke than any of the others. Lea presumed once again he was gathering his thoughts to give a prepared answer or at least think of a way not to give one at all. After a moment, he returned his attention to her and this time gave her a warm smile.

"Technically, as per the mission parameters, I believe you deserve to know absolutely nothing," he said, his smooth and strange accent almost making her believe it. He continued. "But, I suppose I could share a little of what I do with you, without compromising the integrity of my work. I'm sure you appreciate how sensitive these matters can be – we are after all talking about Top Secret governmental business and in this case, it is even more sensitive than usual because this is a bilateral project that is protected under the laws of both the United States and the United Kingdom. I am originally from Finland, but I am permitted inside the project only due to my status as a naturalised British citizen. If I were to say too much, I would of course be prosecuted under the laws of both nations. Heavily. We're talking jail time."

"I'm quite aware of that, Professor," Lea said. "I'm not asking you to divulge anything that's protected or classified in any way. I'm just asking you to give us a summary of your research so that we're able to know exactly what we're getting into here. We're not just bodyguards for the duration of this trip to New York and back. We're a specialist team working for a highly classified international organisation. We have among our number historians, IT specialists, former Special Forces operators – you name it. We're not your run-of-the-mill close protection officers. I don't want to sound arrogant when I say what I'm about to say Professor, but I would be prepared to bet a hefty sum of money that we have handled much more important matters in missions far beyond even your imagination. In this way, you can think of us far above Top Secret."

Obvious curiosity and Lea's comprehensive explanation had this time put an even broader smile on the Finnish professor's face. But then it faded fast.

"It's not just the NDAs, confidentiality agreements and Official Secrets Acts that I have signed on both sides of the Atlantic that concern me Agent Donovan. There are other – shall we say 'agencies' – out there who would do anything to get hold of this information and would play by entirely different rules to do so. Not to mention they would mete out an extremely different kind of punishment if I weren't to conform to their wishes and give them what they wanted."

"Whatever are you saying Professor Haggblom? Lea asked. "I do hope you're not implying that we might be corrupt in some way or hand data to enemy forces."

The professor raised his hands in a gesture of mild surrender. "Not at all, Agent Donovan. I know that you and the rest of your team are extremely reliable and loyal and have protected a great many secrets in your time. However, I'm sure you will appreciate that things can unwind very quickly in certain situations and for that reason the fewer people who know about what I do, the better."

"You're talking about compartmentalization?" Ryan asked.

"Not really," Haggblom said. "There are only two men in the entire world who know about this research and I am one of them. We indeed have assistants and junior researchers working for us, and in this respect, there is some degree of compartmentalization – there has to be for security reasons – but the main core of the research is understood fully only by the two of us."

"That's you and Professor Pinkerton," Hawke said. "The man we're escorting you to meet today in New York City."

"Yes, that's right. Marcus Pinkerton is my research partner. He manages the American side of things and I am on the British side of things, albeit as a proud Finn, although as I say, I took British citizenship many years ago. You might be interested to know that I was required to give up my Finnish citizenship to work on this project, and that is not something I took very lightly at all. The British allow dual citizenship for most things but some things require you to give up your home citizenship. My research was one of them."

"I think the Prime Minister has to be purely British," Scarlet said.

"Well," Haggblom said. "It turns out so do people working in Alpha 6."

"Alpha 6?" Scarlet asked. "I've never heard of that before and I've been around a fair bit."

"This is true," Ryan said. "Ask any dockyard."

"Zip it, cock-knocker," Scarlet immediately shot back.

Noting the look on Haggblom's face, Lea decided to change course back to the subject at hand and also expressed surprise she had never heard of Alpha 6.

"Neither had Sir Richard Eden until a few days ago," Haggblom continued, giving Scarlet a lingering glance. "It's the sixth and highest level above Top Secret. Think UAP-level secrets. There have only ever been forty-three cases of individuals classified at that level since its establishment in 1963."

"In that case, I think we need to know," Scarlet said.

"I'll say!" said Ryan. "Can you confirm UAPs are extraterrestrial?"

Alex sighed.

"I'm not involved with the UAP research at all," Haggblom said.

"That's a shame," Scarlet said, turning to Ryan. "You could have talked to Professor Haggblom about that time you said they probed your — "

"Cairo," Lea said, butting in. "Let's get back to business. I'm sure Professor Haggblom isn't in the mood for your jokes today."

Haggblom tried to return her comment with what Lea supposed he thought was a friendly smile, but he just looked awkward all over again.

"But we still haven't found out exactly what it is you do," Lea asked, pressing him further. "You're being evasive."

Haggblom sighed heavily. "I'm working on a project, codename: Crucible."

Lea glanced at the rest of her teammates and realising no one else was going to speak, asked another question of Haggblom.

"And what is this Crucible, when it's at home?"

"I'm afraid that's pretty much where I have to stop talking," Haggblom said. "I said I wouldn't be able to tell you very much."

"All you've told us is the project you're working on is called Crucible," Lea said. "I think you might be able to give away just a tad more than that."

"We could try Googling it," Ryan said somewhat flippantly.

"You won't find anything about it on Google or anywhere else on the internet," Haggblom said flatly. "The only place the Crucible exists, at least in its full entirety, is in the minds of Professor Pinkerton and myself, and inside my briefcase."

"The one currently handcuffed to your wrist?" Alex asked.

Haggblom nodded. "If it helps you understand the degree of importance and significance of the Crucible, then let me tell you I have not been left alone since I started working on the project seven years ago. During that entire time, I have been permanently accompanied by an armed guard, including even at my home where they sleep in the spare room. They're rotated, permanently on shift."

"They think that you're under that degree of danger?" Alex asked, her eyes widening. "That sounds even worse than what my father had to put up with, and he was the President of the United States."

"Someone at the highest level of government has made that call, Agent Reeve," Haggblom said, his voice tinged with sadness. "But if I want to pursue and perhaps one day complete my research, it is something that I must tolerate. It is part of my life."

Haggblom's eyes started to drift until he was staring blankly into the middle distance, somewhere far outside the plane, and his voice lowered almost to a whisper. "At first, no one could ever truly comprehend what the Crucible would become. Not me, certainly. Funny the way research can do that – outgrow the initial concept – come to dwarf its creator… even threaten its creator."

Here he stopped and looked up to the cabin of the aircraft with a wistful smile on his face, his face brightening, almost as if he was remembering his childhood. "It seems funny to think that when we started, it was just in a regular University Department in Oxford. Marcus and I shared unencrypted emails. Absolute madness. Anyway, it soon became apparent what we were dealing with and then things changed and they changed fast. I was told if I wanted to remain on the project I would sign a raft of forms essentially allowing the government to control the project entirely. As part of the agreement, I would have to tolerate the presence of permanently armed guards. Those were the men you saw in my Volvo. They drove me to the airport. They cannot work in the United States for legal reasons, as they are British government agents. So now you are taking me across to New York, where after I meet with Marcus you will escort me back to the airport and there my armed guards will pick me up and take me back either to my office or my home. That is my life. That is the life I must lead since creating the Crucible."

Alex leaned forward, officially intrigued. "But what exactly *is* the Crucible? Some kind of nuclear device?"

Haggblom gave her a polite, almost fatherly smile and shook his head gently. "It's far more dangerous than a nuclear device, Agent Reeve. The Crucible, if ever unleashed, would have the power not only to cause every bit as much damage as a nuclear device, and almost certainly significantly more but to affect almost every single human being on the planet, even those far away from its deployment and within no more than a few minutes. There would be no way back – no way to reverse its release, no way to stop its devastating effects on humanity."

"And that fucking thing is sitting on your lap right now?" Scarlet asked.

"It is indeed," Haggblom said. "And one day you might understand why I have to make this journey in person and not simply communicate to Marcus in the usual ways – even using encrypted technology. Far too dangerous you see. It's far too dangerous. Even an encrypted message could be intercepted. I couldn't live with it. Perhaps one day we may be able to engineer the Crucible in such a way that it becomes useful to humanity, but for now, it is in its infancy, and it is not something that we want raging around the world creating havoc."

Lea sat back in her seat, convinced Haggblom had said all he was going to say. She had failed to get anything more out of him and now Alex had tried and also failed. She still had no idea what was inside the briefcase handcuffed to Haggblom's wrist. She didn't even know how heavy it was and no one had been allowed to touch it since they had picked him up back at Heathrow.

Outside the starboard window, Lea now saw the coast of Galway and Connemara – her homeland – slowly disappearing out of sight behind the aircraft as the plane continued cruising across the Atlantic on its way to their final destination. For now, at least, she would have to contain her intrigue and go back to the basic parameters of her mission – protecting Professor Haggblom and what she now knew was called the Crucible.

CHAPTER SEVEN

DC ran the Cayman Crew. He was an old hand with a trail of destruction in his wake, gnarled, leathery hands and as the old saying went, a face like a welder's bench. He'd burnt up the best years of his life as a Delta Force soldier until a dishonourable discharge, for reasons known only to himself, three years ago. He hated most things in life and he only liked things it was wrong to like.

Then there was Cambridge. Cambridge joined the crew after being thrown out of the British Army for theft and drug offences. He was ex-Regiment. SAS. Cambridge was DC's Right-Hand Man and knew every trick in the book, especially if that book was about special military tactics and asymmetrical warfare.

Next in line was Paris, a French brunette who had been ejected from the DGES, France's equivalent of MI6 or CIA, also for reasons unknown to anyone but herself. Tall and slim and elegant when she had to be, her true side was darker than the inside of a Black Hole. She was the quietest member of the crew and preferred always to listen rather than talk.

Moscow was sitting beside DC. She was a stocky, blonde Russian woman who had served in the Russian Army, specifically the Motorised Rifle Division. She was built like a T-34 tank and never showed any fear, no matter what came at her. Truth was, she probably unnerved DC more than anyone else on the team.

Then there was Haifa. The Israeli Defence Forces had invited Haifa to leave after she had hacked into their payroll and given herself a substantial pay rise, even larger than the Chief of Staff's salary. She spent her time inside the world of computers and anything related to them, smoked like a Victorian chimney. After her expulsion from the IDF, the dark-eyed young woman had found a new family in the form of DC's crew.

"How are we going, Haifa?"

She nodded once, eyes never leaving the screen. "Almost there, DC."

Dresden sucked his teeth. "And you said that five minutes ago. Hurry up."

They were sitting in the back of a van. Sitting behind the steering wheel, the blonde Russian woman, named

Samara after her hometown, stared at Dresden in the mirror and scowled. "She's hacking into the airport and tracking passports, stuff a moron like you could never dream of doing. If you shut up, she could work even faster. Haven't you got a squeaky toy to play with?"

Paris laughed, and muttered under breath, "C'est vrai, Dresden, espèce de connard."

"I heard that," Dresden said. "You think just because I blow things up all day long, I can't speak any French?"

"Take it easy, Dresden," DC said.

"She called me an asshole."

DC fixed his gaze on the German. "That's because you are an asshole."

Dresden slumped into his seat, disgruntled, and fired up a cigarette.

DC also leaned back, but a look of steely determination appeared in his eyes. "Everyone just take it easy. We're nearly there. Then this can all be over and we're done. But in the meantime, we stay focused and alert. I want Haggblom. We must get Haggblom. When we have him, we have the Crucible."

Silence fell over the inside of the GMC van like a heavy fog. Only DC had the authority to break it. "And when we have the Crucible, we have the world."

Or at least that's what he'd been told by the Director. As it was, DC was a regular US Army Infantryman whose great survival skills and extreme calmness under fire and stamina had enabled him to rise into the ranks of the US Delta Force, but he was no expert in cutting-edge scientific research and doomsday weapons. He was the leader of the muscle team, the men in the field, the boots on the ground that made things happen. Without the boots on the ground, nothing ever happened, he knew that from all the places he'd been deployed as a regular soldier and a Delta Force operator. Ideas could be as high and mighty as you like, but nothing ever happened until the boots got on the ground.

Right now his boots were on the ground in New York City, more specifically in the footwell of a GMC panel van parked up in lower Manhattan on a cold day with snow whipping around in front of the windscreen. The engine wasn't on, so the heater wasn't on. Sure his feet were cold, but they were inside those boots he'd just been thinking about, and no man of his military experience and training was going to ever be bothered about a few cold toes. All that was on DC's mind was the successful execution of the immediate mission – which in this case meant the apprehension of a strangely named professor, and most important of all – as the Director had said – the acquisition of a steel briefcase that was handcuffed to their target's wrist.

The Director had not gone into specifics about what was inside the briefcase or exactly who this Haggblom was or what he knew, but he had found the time to say that if he wouldn't come quietly, he was to hack off his hand and take the briefcase. While Haggblom was important, the Director had made it crystal clear that the briefcase was more important. DC had faith they could deliver. They had been highly successful and desirable mercenaries-for-hire for many years now and had done all manner of dirty deeds for the highest bidder. Hacking off a man's hand to steal a briefcase would not present a problem for anyone on board his crew. Then he could hand over the briefcase to the Director, a strange figure whose acquaintance he'd never had the pleasure of knowing, and the organisation he ran, a group called the Midnight Syndicate.

DC had not the first idea who the Midnight Syndicate were. That was always the arrangement with those who hired the crew – no unnecessary questions would be asked, so no awkward answers needed to be given. A nice, simple business arrangement, that was what DC liked. They got hired, they got paid, and everyone went home happy. Apart from Mrs Haggblom, he guessed. His crew had worked for everyone from Colombian drug lords, to African warlords and everything in between. He had helped traffic drugs and weapons into and out of the United States. He had helped rescue hostages taken by Somali Pirates. He had killed corrupt CIA officers and agents who had tortured people. He had snatched Mafia men off the streets and buried them in the foundations of new suburban divisions out of the city. There was no good or bad in business – there were no ethics. DC never turned down a job, so long as the pay was right. And in this case, the pay was better than right.

The Midnight Syndicate had offered him more money than they had ever been paid for any previous jobs, they had offered so much money that it amounted to more than the last seven jobs they had done all added up together. The sum of cash that the Midnight Syndicate offered to

DC and his team was so great that DC had quickly calculated that he would be able to make it his last job and retire to a small island he knew somewhere near Costa Rica. It was a small, uninhabited island – just the kind of place that he wanted to spend the rest of his retirement in, counting crypto and reliving his most daring exploits. He'd already started dreaming of the villa he would build there, complete with a Bali-hut hot tub and views of the beach. He would build a jetty to moor a seaplane, which he was more than capable of piloting having been trained to fly in the military. What happened to the rest of the team was their fucking business. They would be paid fairly and then they could get lost. It was all good.

"How much longer until he's here?"

It was Paris, speaking from behind him in the van. She had just finished disassembling and reassembling one of her weapons. "Because it's pretty cold back here and I'm getting bored."

DC smirked when he heard the French woman complaining, but knew she was being sarcastic. Everyone on the team including Paris had sustained significantly more deprivation and hardship than an hour or two in a cold van parked up in New York City.

"I don't care about the cold," Dresden said. "But I want something to eat. Do you think that street vendor over there would put three or four patties in a burger bun for me?"

"This is America," Cambridge said. "I think they'd be disappointed at anything less than three or four burgers in a bun."

"In answer to your question, Paris," DC said, his voice level, "And overlooking that slight about my homeland from the Limey here, the target should be here within the next half hour. When they land, our second team will attack the two LLVs, led by Miami and Havana. They will snatch Haggblom and bring him to us and we will then take him to the Director. Simple. We will not be turning the engine on and alleviating cold feet, and no one will be leaving the van to buy burgers. Is that clear?"

There was a murmur of grim laughter coming from the back of the van and now DC turned to Moscow, the Russian woman who was sitting up front beside him in the passenger seat. She was sucking on a Russian cigarette and had said almost nothing since they had pulled up and switched the engine off. Now she turned to him and offered him a cigarette.

"No thanks," DC said, waving it away.

"I always smoke when I need to calm down," she said in a heavy Russian accent. "Or when I'm about to kill someone."

"Talking of which," Haifa said. "Rio and Paolo did some good work in Rio. They're trying to upstage me."

DC checked his watch again. "They're not upstaging anyone. I gave them a job to do and they did well. Now we have some insurance. But forget about them. I don't want it to bleed into this mission. Rio and Paolo did good work, and now it's our turn. We keep our eye on the ball in play right here in New York. Everyone clear on that?"

He saw a round of head nods and knew everyone was all clear. He checked his watch and settled down for the last few minutes. Soon, things would move as fast as lightning.

CHAPTER EIGHT

Lea Donovan gazed peacefully through the Gulfstream's window as it banked on its final approach to JFK airport. She seemed to spend the major part of her life airborne these days and had done so for many years. It seemed odd to have to fly from Colorado to London and then back to New York but that was the only way they could complete their mission to successfully protect Professor Haggblom. She was wondering whether they should fly back to Colorado at the end after dropping their charge back in London, or perhaps go straight down to Elysium and turn their attention back to work because as far as she was concerned, the ECHO team still had outstanding business.

She was thinking of the white-robed guardians of the Land of the Gods.

These strange warriors had appeared out of nowhere in the ancient structure they had found in the Land of the Gods called the Citadel, and fought valiantly in defence of the place before retreating and leaving them no clue as to who they were. She knew they were not Athanatoi and they were certainly not regular Special Forces or any ground army of any kind. No – those men and women who had appeared out of nowhere in the Citadel were part of something else and she was determined to find out who. They certainly wouldn't be able to do that playing on the ski slopes and drinking in the cosy bars of Telluride.

With the thought of the Citadel in mind, she decided to return the team to Elysium after the mission and decided she would try to persuade Richard Eden to release the funds to research the white-robed guardians. She would also call Ravi and Kahlia in Rio and have them return to the private Caribbean island at the same time, bringing the entire team together. They had lost many good friends and comrades over the years, sometimes in the most unimaginably awful and brutal circumstances, so she was very grateful to be alive and thankful that the rest of her team was alive and fit and healthy. An ECHO comrade hadn't fallen since Lexi Zhang, also known by her Chinese assassin codename 'Dragonfly' at the hands of King Kashala's mercenaries at his compound deep in the Congo. Lexi's death had scarred the team bitterly, but she had sensed in the last few days they were beginning to move on. Lexi's name was mentioned less and less in conversation, which while sad on one hand, was a good thing on the other. Lea wanted to direct the attention of the surviving team members to complete their Athanatoi mission and find out who the white-robed guardians were, even if this would take time and resources away from more immediate and pressing missions that never seemed to stop coming their way.

She sighed and re-arranged her position in the small aircraft seat.

Was it all worth it?

She never doubted it. After her father's mysterious disappearance so many years ago, Sir Richard Eden had taken her under his wing and changed her life in ways unimaginable to most people. She had travelled the world, visiting every continent and a good number of the planet's countries as well. She had been to the Arctic Circle, she had fought on the snowy plains and mountains of Antarctica. She had sweltered under Africa's fierce savanna sun and traversed the treacherous streets of some of the most dangerous cities in the world, all in the name of fighting the good fight and putting evil down wherever she found it.

But there had been a price.

Although she had once been married to Ryan and was now engaged to Hawke, her lifestyle had meant never being able to properly settle down, do the things that other young women her age did, lead a normal life in a normal job and look forward to Friday nights, going out with her friends at the weekends into the city to enjoy a drink or a show, settle down with a man, start a family. She supposed there was a chance of that now with Hawke, but neither of them was getting any younger and she knew this would mean leaving ECHO. There was no way she could bring up her child in an environment like this, not just because of the everyday dangers he or she would face, but how did you explain to your child that you were an international freedom fighter, ranging the world to take down evil megalomaniacs and doomsday weapons? Maybe this was something you could tell a teenager, but certainly not a younger child.

None of that mattered for now – for now she had a job to do, just like every other week in her life, and she marshalled her usual attentive focus on the specific purpose of the goal of transporting Haggblom to his mysterious conference with Professor Pinkerton and bringing him home safely again. She was ready. She settled back in her seat and enjoyed the descent over the eastern reaches of the United States. Soon they would be landing in New York City.

CHAPTER NINE

After being hurried through US Customs, the team located the vehicle arranged by Eden and were soon on the road. They turned onto Manhattan Bridge and drove slowly north in a long line of traffic. Hawke was sitting behind Reaper who was driving, and was able to see the Brooklyn Bridge to their west, and beyond it, the Financial District's skyscrapers sparkling in the afternoon sun. A few scattered clouds did little to spoil the mainly blue sky, and it felt like a different world from the wet, grey gloom of London a few hours ago.

He checked his watch. They were running behind by half an hour due to a delay when they were stacked to get into JFK, but nothing too bad. He was satisfied all was going to plan and they would soon reach the halfway mark in their mission: escorting Haggblom to a secret US Government Research Facility in Lower Manhattan.

Reaper drove off the bridge and continued in the same direction until bearing left onto Canal Street. Suddenly, he turned right onto Elizabeth Street causing Haggblom to look up from the papers in his briefcase. "What's happening?"

"Someone has been tailing us since we got on the bridge," Reaper said. "I'm just taking some extra precautions. Relax and go back to your work."

"You think it could be trouble?" Haggblom asked nervously.

"I doubt it," Hawke said. "But it's better to be safe than sorry."

Hawke leaned in between the two front seats, shuffling forward as far as he could safely go, and exchanged a glance with Reaper, and then with Scarlet who was sitting to the Frenchman's right in the front passenger seat. Hawke broke off his gaze with her and followed their progress on the onboard satnav display system.

"Which way are you going to go now?" he asked Reaper.

"Just going around one block ought to see if he's following us. I'll turn left onto Hester Street and then south on Mott before turning right back onto Canal Street and rejoining our original route. No one would ever take that route to get to Lafayette Street."

As Reaper spoke, Scarlet leaned forward and opened the glove box. Without a word, she leaned forward and reached inside, pulling out six Glock 19s and the same number of concealed carry belt clips. She handed them around. Hawke and Lea took theirs under the unsettled gaze of Haggblom, Alex and Ryan were at the back of the SUV, and leaned forward to take theirs while upfront, Scarlet placed Reaper's on the central consul. Then she handed around six fresh magazines, each fully loaded and ready to go. With the sound of the mags being fixed into the guns' grips, Hawke leaned back into his seat and gave Lea a conspiratorial wink.

"All good?"

"I guess so. That guy still on our asses?"

Scarlet checked her mirror and answered before Hawke had a chance to turn in his seat.

"Affirmative."

Alex and Ryan turned and checked through the window behind them, confirming.

Hawke now looked instinctively over his shoulder, his eyes staring down over Haggblom's shoulder and through the SUV's rear window. Although most of this window was covered in the usual dirty slush caused by road salt and snow, a neat horseshoe of clean glass had been cleared by the rear wiper. Hawke peered through this section and saw the car, a filthy titanium-grey GMC Yukon cruising menacingly behind them, three cars back, its gloss-black ABS plastic grille concealing a 6.2 Litre Vortec engine. More than up to the job.

Hawke watched the Yukon for a full minute and then turned his attention to the road. Reaper was now indicating left and preparing to turn the SUV onto Lafayette Street when the lights changed to red and forced the Frenchman to slow to a stop. Hawke took another look around. They were now parallel to Canal Street Subway Station in a dense gridlock of traffic waiting to move on. The blue sky began to darken, with clouds slowly rolling in from the north, threatening to bring with it more cold and snow from further upstate and beyond in Canada. The temperature in the car dropped. Reaper adjusted the heater, then he adjusted his beanie and calmly studied his handlebar moustache in the mirror for a few seconds.

"It's going much greyer," he said without emotion.

"You need a shave," Scarlet said. "You look like a Mexican bandit."

"In that case, I certainly will not shave," he said.

The lights stayed red. It began to snow. In response to the drop in temperature, the air around the cars outside grew colder and denser, causing the exhaust gases to condense in the atmosphere and turn into ice crystals at a much faster rate. Hawke watched the thick new clouds of exhaust vapour rising from the cars in front, forming a kind of smog in front of their SUV. Reaper put the wipers on intermittent.

"We're tucked in too tight," Alex said from the rear.

"I'm not happy either, Joe," Lea said. "We're fish in a barrel."

Haggblom regarded Lea with furrowed brows. He slowly closed his briefcase and the little metallic click filled the cabin. "What does that mean?"

"It means keep quiet and let us do the thinking," Scarlet said.

Hawke's instinct began to bother him. The moment fell quiet. The atmosphere in the car thickened. Something was off. Scarlet felt it too. Her eyes were fixed to the side mirror and she pulled her Glock out of her belt clip.

Up ahead, above the cars, Hawke watched the lights change to green through the cloud of exhaust fumes and falling snow. The cars in front of them began to trundle forward, some going left, some right and some straight ahead. Reaper reactivated the left-hand indication signal and gently put his foot down on the accelerator pedal, nudging the SUV forward. As he reached the crosswalk, he began to turn the steering wheel to the left and aimed the car for the slow lane of Lafayette Street.

And then Hawke saw a boxy US Postal Service van racing out of Walker Street, ahead of them on their left. It took him a few seconds to contemplate if the van was a threat or merely a legitimate US postal worker whose vehicle was out of control. But as the famous Long Life Vehicle or LLV, now turned sharply to its right and headed straight for their SUV, it was obvious it was a threat and they were the target.

"Look out!" Hawke yelled.

Reaper had already seen the threat and responded to it before the words had left Hawke's lips. He was now steering hard to the right in an attempt to avoid a collision with the LLV but was forced to cut up a vehicle behind them in the fast lane as he did it, just catching the front of the other vehicle, crunching its front left bumper and forcing it over onto the right on the pavement. In a hail of blaring car horns and rage, the driver now climbed out of his wrecked car and began shouting and screaming at the ECHO team.

No one inside the SUV gave a damn. The LLV had rapidly corrected course and was driving at full speed into their front left crunching the SUV's front left wing, buckling its front left tyre and snapping it off the axle. The impact slammed their nose abruptly to the right, forcing the SUV through the fast lane and onto the pavement on the west side of Lafayette Street. All their airbags instantly exploded in their faces, knocking Scarlet's gun from her hand and inciting a volley of unspeakable French swear words from Reaper, who now swiped the deflating airbag out of his way before reaching down for his Glock on the central console. It was no longer there. The impact had knocked it from the console down into the gap between the console and Scarlet's seat. Now Scarlet also pushed her deflating airbag out of her face and was reaching down into her footwell to find the Glock. At the same time, Reaper finally located the weapon from the gap between the console and the seat.

In the back, the others were all ready with their weapons, all now gripped securely in their hands. Lea had already forced Haggblom's head down into the seat to keep him out of the line of fire, at the same time Hawke had kicked open his door, unclipped his belt and was now out of the SUV, his gun raised into the aim and walking at a fast pace towards the LLV which had been badly damaged in the attack. Alex and Ryan climbed out and took up defensive positions around Haggblom as Hawke marched towards the LLV. Steam was billowing from its bonnet and Hawke could see the driver was slumped over the steering wheel inside the vehicle's cab.

The man inside the cab began to stir. Hawke was already training his attention on the back of the LLV but now swung his Glock to the right and fired three shots through the driver's window, killing him instantly. He did this without slowing down his journey on the way to the back of the LLV and now swung his weapon back around to neutralise any threat that might be in the back of the LLV postal van.

He heard the LLV's two rear doors swing open and crash against the van's exterior before he saw it. Two men had climbed out of the back of the LLV and were now walking around either side, one coming towards him and the other walking around the far side of the vehicle.

Hawke had not yet seen the man on the far side of the van, but the man who was now in front of him was wearing full black combat fatigues and a black balaclava obscured his face. He was carrying a compact submachine gun that Hawke instantly recognised as an MP5.

Hawke's Glock was already raised and pointing at the man. He squeezed the trigger and fired two shots into his head and one into his heart in a faction of a second, before the man even had a chance to raise his weapon. Hawke now moved rapidly to the rear of the van before spinning around with his gun raised and checking that the back of the van was clear of any further threat.

"Clear!" he yelled.

But he knew that the other man who had exited the vehicle was now running around the front of the LLV on the way to their SUV. Hawke now fell to the ground and lying flat on the cold snowy concrete, he followed a pair of black riot boots as they made their way towards the SUV. Hawke fired, aiming for the man's boots, but he had already moved out of sight behind the crunched up front of their vehicle. Hawke spoke into his palm mic. "He's heading your way. Anyone reading me?"

Lea came back first. "I'm here Joe. We see you."

"You should be able to take him out there's only one left!"

"That's old news, baby," Scarlet said. "A second postal van just pulled up on our right. Another three guys just joined the fun."

"It gets worse," Hawke said, still in his position down on the pavement as he watched the man's combat boots come back into view. He watched carefully as the mercenary crouched and fitted a magnetised bomb to the bottom of the SUV.

"You've gotta get out of the car, Scarlet! Lea? Did you hear me? Anyone left in the SUV has got to get out now!"

Hawke fired on the combat boots a second time but they sprinted away behind the second postal van. He jumped to his feet and ran around the side of the LLV, the same way he had come and was instantly met by a barrage of rounds fired from the new mercenaries who had now taken cover behind the second LLV van. He threw himself on the ground and tried to roll under their vehicle to remove the magnetised bomb, but he couldn't get close enough without being hit by the mercenaries' bullets.

"I can't get the bomb off! Everybody out!"

He heard the doors of the SUV open and then saw his teammates who had stayed inside the van with Haggblom as they jumped from the vehicle. Then he saw Haggblom's expensive loafers as Lea dragged him away from the SUV. Hawke jumped to his feet again and supported Reaper and Scarlet in their bid to provide cover fire for Lea as she tried to drag Haggblom into a side street on the west side of Lafayette.

Whoever these guys were, they were acting with serious speed and lethality. Hawke now heard a scream and turned to see what looked like a woman, although it was hard to tell through the black combat fatigues, effortlessly disarming Lea and driving the grip of her weapon into her temple, instantly knocking her down. Haggblom stood terrified and defenceless and now raised his hands in surrender, the left one still handcuffed to his steel briefcase.

Still under heavy fire from the men arranged in cover positions around the back of the second LLV postal van, Hawke, Reaper and Scarlet were unable to get to Lea to offer assistance and now Hawke watched helplessly as the woman who had knocked Lea out now dragged Haggblom out of sight around the corner into Walker

Street. The next thing he heard was the sound of doors slamming and then the wild revving of a powerful engine. At the same time, the newly arrived mercenaries who were taking cover behind the second postal van now perforated their SUV until it looked like Swiss cheese, driving Alex and Ryan back behind the cover of another vehicle as their SUV collapsed down sadly on blown-out tyres.

Then the bomb under the SUV detonated and created an enormous fireball in the middle of the street, driving everyone further back. Hawke shielded his face from the heat of the blast. The mercenaries stepped back along Lafayette, firing incessantly from their compact machine pistols as they went until they rendezvoused with a black GMC panel van at the end of the block, presumably the same vehicle the woman had used to flee with Haggblom. It screeched down White Street and then they were gone.

Staring at both postal vans, which had been given nearly as much of a beating as their SUV until its detonation, Hawke could barely believe what he had just seen. Turning to the others, including Lea who was now on her feet and walking over to them, he felt his world collapsing inwards. All around him, he heard the cacophonous roaring of emergency service sirens approaching from both directions of Lafayette Street.

Hawke could find no words but merely shrugged in desperation.

Scarlet was the first to speak.

"Well… we fucked that right up, didn't we?"

CHAPTER TEN

Less than an hour later, Hawke and his comrades were gathered around Lea's phone, which was propped up against a potted plant in a hotel room in the New York Marriott Marquis on the northwest corner of Times Square. They had successfully evaded the police who had raced to the scene within a few short minutes in response to the shooting on Lafayette Street, but no one felt very good about themselves. To say they were suffering from a severe case of wounded pride was an understatement.

Seeing the look on Richard Eden's face, on Lea's phone screen, did not help matters much.

"What the hell just happened out there?" Eden barked.

"What happened was we weren't properly briefed about how dangerous this mission was going to be," Scarlet said in her usual forthright way.

For a second Eden looked like he was about to explode. Hawke took note – this was extremely uncharacteristic of their boss.

"There were seven of them," Lea said, trying to dissipate the tension on the call. "No, there were at *least* seven of them. Three in each vehicle and at least one in a GMC van. At this time we can't be sure if the woman who nearly knocked me out was also the driver of the GMC, although I strongly suspect there would have been another person inside the GMC waiting for her to bring Haggblom back to it."

Eden peered forward towards his screen and winced. "That looks like a hell of a bruise you've got there, Lea. Are you sure you're OK to continue this mission?"

"I'm fine."

As she spoke, she began to sway and reached out for the table to help her balance. Hawke also reached out to her and steadied her.

"I'd be happier if you got some hospital attention before going forward," Eden said. "Head injuries can be serious."

"I agree," Hawke said.

She sighed. "I said I'm fine. I've been through much worse."

"I trust your judgement," Eden said.

"Me too," Hawke added.

"Back to the mission," Eden said, his face darkening. "I've already reported the kidnapping of Professor Haggblom to the same Ministry of Defence official who got in contact with me about this mission in the first place. As you can imagine, he is extremely displeased with this most unfortunate turn of events and requires an immediate resolution to it in his favour, and that is exactly how he put it."

"What he means is, sort this fucking shitshow out right now and get Haggblom back, am I right?" Scarlet asked.

"Succinctly put, Cairo," Eden said.

"Well, we've done it before and we can do it again," Hawke said. "And when we catch up with the bastards who did this, we've got a big score to settle especially for punching Lea like that." He reached across and put his arm around her, giving her a gentle hug.

"I agree," Reaper said. "It should be easy enough once we've got a good lead."

"I don't think it's going to be easy enough at all," Eden said. "In my conversation with the Ministry of Defence official who by now you will have worked out is going to remain anonymous throughout this process, he gave me more information about Haggblom's work. I got the sense he was still keeping an awful lot to himself, but he was still keeping almost everything a secret, he has included me on some of the more important essentials. Haggblom and Pinkerton are working on a creation called The Crucible."

"Haggblom already told us that," Alex said.

"Did he say anything else?" Eden asked.

Everyone shook their heads.

"Same here," Eden continued. "My contact was very vague about exactly what the Crucible is, but he managed to find the words in his vocabulary to tell me that it is a weapon of unimaginable power and not only that but of an unimaginable *type*. That is what he said. He told me that it was a weapon I couldn't possibly imagine. He made no further clarification on the matter. I don't like it, especially since Haggblom fell into the hands of these mercenaries today."

"Well, that sounds bloody smashing," Scarlet said. "Oh, and by the way – why the fucking hell didn't they tell us this before we took the job on?"

"I agree with Scarlet," Reaper said. "You told us – because they told you – that this was a fairly routine mission escorting a scientist across the Atlantic so he could attend a meeting in what was described as a very secure environment. Then we find out about this Crucible. If they had told us this in the first place, we could have made better arrangements and possibly avoided any of this happening at all."

"Concurred," Eden said. "But now is not the time to go over any of this. We can go over the 'coulds and woulds' when all of this is over. For now, you must retrieve Haggblom and the research in his briefcase."

"Is Pinkerton okay?" Hawke asked.

"We're looking into it," Eden said.

Lea frowned. "Wait, these bastards didn't get the Crucible itself – they just got Haggblom and his research, is that right?"

Eden nodded. "Not sure, but I believe so. The MOD official refused to speak any further on the matter of The Crucible beyond simply telling me what I've already told you – that it is a highly dangerous weapon of an entirely unimaginable kind, different to anything that currently exists in the world and that it is of vital national importance to the United States and the United Kingdom that both the contents of the briefcase and Haggblom are retrieved. And here's another thing, the…"

"Er, guys," Reaper said, interrupting. "You might want to take a look at this."

Hawke walked over to him and stared down at one of the enormous LED billboards in Times Square, far below their hotel room. Haggblom's face was now filling the billboard, and he was holding up a note written in a fat black marker pen on a white card: "We have the Crucible. We want three more things."

"Are you seeing this, Rich?" Lea asked, pointing her phone camera at the billboard.

Eden's face was like granite. "I'm seeing it."

Hawke stared at the billboard and worked hard to keep his composure.

A terrified Haggblom now looked off camera for a moment before dropping the first card to reveal a second one with a new message, also written in black marker pen.

"Number #1: the President of the United States will resign."

Haggblom showed the third card.

"Number #2: we require $50 billion in Bitcoin transferred to the place of our choosing."

And a fourth card: "Number #3: we require the release of Khalid Al-Harazi."

And a fifth and final card: "You have 24 hours to meet all three of these demands or Haggblom will be executed and the Crucible will be deployed against the United States. We'll be in touch. Have a nice day!" Below the message was a smiling emoji. Then, Haggblom's face faded away and an advert for milkshakes appeared in giant flashing technicolour.

The crowds in Times Square panicked and bolted in all directions.

"Well," Scarlet said, "Shit in my hat and punch it. That's a new one for me."

"And who said the aristocracy was above the rest of us?" Lea said, looking at Scarlet.

"I want to know how they hacked into that billboard," Hawke said, as the terrified mass of people below continued to stream out of Times Square.

"Well, that's a coincidence, Joe, because I want to know too," Eden said, barely concealing his anger. "I also want to know who snatched Haggblom and where they're holding him. And I want to know all of this yesterday. After this every alphabet agency on Earth will be all over it like white on rice. They're big and many of their agents could be compromised in some way, so I want you to fix this, not them. Get on with it."

Neither Hawke nor anyone else on the team needed to be told twice.

They were at war again.

CHAPTER ELEVEN

As Reaper scanned the television news stories to see how the kidnapping and Times Square spectacles were being received around America and the rest of the world, Scarlet was getting nowhere trying to reach Kahlia or Ravi down in South America. Alex and Ryan, whom Scarlet called 'Team Nerd' had already begun working on the problem.

"Whoever hacked into the LED billboard on Times Square was good. They left no trace whatsoever," Alex said. "But we were able to run the licence plates of the GMC van, which I was able to retrieve from hacking into the New York City CCTV system, using one of the cameras on Lafayette and Walker. The GMC van is owned by a shell company registered in the Cayman Islands. Unfortunately, there the well kind of runs dry, but I did manage to get a small lead."

"Thank God for that," Lea said, starting to sound exasperated.

"What did you find, Alex?" Hawke asked.

"I already contacted a CIA contact of mine who lives on the islands. He has cooperated with the Caymanian authorities in the past and he filed a request to obtain records connected to the shell company. There was only one name on the paperwork and that was Franklin Claremont."

"And what do we know about Franklin Claremont?" Hawke asked. "Except he sounds like he owns a vineyard."

Alex smiled. "He doesn't own a vineyard, that's for damn sure. Franklin P. Claremont was a highly decorated American Special Forces soldier working inside the Delta Force. He notched up some serious experience around the world, including in Afghanistan and Iraq before being unceremoniously booted out of the force and the US military in general with a dishonourable discharge. Now he runs an outfit of mercenaries called the Cayman Crew. I can't say exactly who this guy is, but I'd say he's probably the head honcho of the team that snatched Haggblom."

"And the briefcase," Ryan said.

"And the briefcase, sure," Alex said.

Hawke felt a surge of excitement and optimism. "That's great work, Alex. We've got a name – Franklin Claremont – and he's former Delta Force which would explain some of those moves we saw back on Lafayette Street."

"Do we know anything else about the identities of the Cayman Crew?" Lea asked.

"They have good taste in locations for their shell companies?" Ryan said.

As Scarlet was slapping the back of his head, Lea went on. "As Rich said, we need to know about these guys. Today they just kidnapped a scientist and what we now understand is one of the world's most dangerous weapons from right under our noses. Then they somehow managed to hack into an LED Billboard on Times Square and make the most outrageous demands I've ever heard of by way of a ransom – the resignation of the President of the United States, $50 billion of Bitcoin, and the release of One of Yemen's most dangerous mercenary warlords."

"You know who that Al-Harazi dude was?" Ryan asked.

"It's my business to know," Lea said. "Sorry, I didn't mean that the way it came out."

Ryan waved it away. "Forget about it."

Hawke said, "This is a good point though, you think the Cayman Crew are working with Al-Harazi? Is he bankrolling them? And what is it they want – a political outcome such as the President of the US being forced to resign, or is this just a glorified bank job which is why they want the 50 billion in Bitcoin?"

"Some kind of Die Hard sleight of hand?" Ryan asked. "I like it."

"Maybe," Hawke said. "It's got me confused. Are they simply freelance mercenaries?"

"Mercenaries R Us?" Alex said.

"And don't forget this sodding Crucible," Scarlet said. "At the heart of all of this is probably the biggest fucking ticking timebomb any of us could ever dream of."

A long silence.

"I'm with Lea," Hawke said.

"We all know that Big Guy," Ryan said, slapping him on his back. "When's the Big Day?"

"I meant…"

Ryan laughed. "I know what you meant, Joe."

Hawke smiled, but it faded fast. "These guys seemed to want odd things as part of their ransom. Planning this operation must have meant a huge amount of trouble for them, not to mention considerable resources and logistics and great all-round risk. Okay, so they pulled it off and they've got Haggblom and his research but then they go and risk being caught again by leaving a trail of digital breadcrumbs behind them when they hack into the LED Billboard. Does not make sense."

"But the breadcrumbs end abruptly, Joe," Alex said. "They knew they were capable of hacking into it with no risk to themselves. And don't underestimate Claremont, from the research I've already done on him, he's one of the most violent and aggressive criminal masterminds we've ever crossed paths with. In between his time as a Delta Force soldier and starting up the Cayman Crew, he worked in a bank robbery outfit called The Cleaners in Atlantic City. On one of their raids, he mowed down a young family of four – a mother, father and two young girls, when he was on his way out of the bank after the raid because his mask slipped and one of the little girls saw his face. He's not the kind of guy you mess with lightly."

"Bastard," Ryan said.

"I told Haggblom he wasn't in any danger," Lea said with regret. "That's not the kind of thing I want to live with. I saw the look on his face when those bastards started shooting at us. I want him back. Unharmed."

"Yes, and I want the bloody Crucible or whatever the hell is in that case, back too," Scarlet said. "These tossers might not want to tell us what it is, but I'm not liking the sound of an unimaginable weapon. Sounds like the kind of thing that's gonna suck all of the air out of the Earth's atmosphere or something."

"Well, it can't be that," Hawke said.

She turned on him. "Why the fuck not?"

"Because you just imagined it."

After a long silence, he said, "Let's get moving. We have a job to do, and this time it's exactly what we do best. But we need to move fast because time is of the essence on this mission, and if…"

Hawke stopped talking abruptly when he saw a strange look on Lea's face. She had been staring down at her phone screen and he'd guessed that she was trying to find another lead. Instead, her face turned ashen white and her hands were beginning to tremble.

"Lea? What the hell's the matter?" he asked.

She looked at him, her eyes sad and desperate with fear. She turned and looked at Scarlet and Reaper in the same way and then turned and lifted her phone so they were all able to see the screen. It was an incoming Zoom call, And the caller ID section was three simple words: The Cayman Crew.

CHAPTER TWELVE

Lea's phone rang again, drawing her attention back to the incoming Zoom call.

"Why the hell are they calling us?" she said.

"Maybe they've branched out into deliveries," Scarlet said. "Anyone order anything to be delivered? A pizza for me and Reap? A book from Amazon for Alex. A gimp suit for Ryan?"

The joke didn't lighten the mood. Lea hesitated, not sure how to respond. She looked at Hawke. He gestured for her to take the call. She agreed and was now face-to-face with the enemy.

"Hello Lea, this is Franklin Claremont. My friends call me DC."

Lea had rarely felt so creeped out and then when she heard his voice, and saw the blank look in his eyes. A cold, hard, calculation was the only thing they gave off, no emotion at all. She knew the best way to fight evil was head-on, so she straightened herself up, cleared her throat, and spoke in a clear level voice not displaying a hint of fear.

"What do you want, Claremont?"

"If you answer my riddle, then maybe I might tell you. Are you ready to answer my riddle?"

"If that's what I have to do."

"Yes, I rather feel it is what you have to do, Agent Donovan. Because I'm calling the shots now, aren't I? Not you and the rest of your high and mighty ECHO team, but me. Yes, that's right, I know all about you and everything you've done. My employers are very powerful people and believe in giving their contracted workforce a full briefing before sending them into the field."

Lea felt a shiver go up her spine. He had referred to 'his employers'. That meant he was working for someone else, someone else was calling the shots. That made everything ten times worse.

DC went on. "I know all about Dickie Eden, you and your beloved Connemara, Major Hawke and his parkour – aren't you getting on a little bit for that sort of carry-on, Josiah? I never saw anyone with a paunch do parkour before."

Scarlet leaned into Hawke and lowered her voice to a whisper. "Look, I know he's an obvious creep Joe, but he has got a point on that one."

Hawke gave her a sideways look but said nothing, returning his attention to the cold voice speaking over the phone speaker.

"I know all about you too, Scarlet Sloane and your brother Spencer the good little Baronet sitting in his little mansion back in England. Aristocrats, no less. I am honoured. And it gets better. I'm in no less company than the daughter of a former President of the United States, Alex Reeve. You're slumming things a bit aren't you, Alex? I mean, dating a pathetic, sad little loser like Ryan Bale? And how are the legs? I have it on very good authority you need a potion to stay standing up. That sucks. And then we have a big, tough former French Legionnaire, Vincent Reno. The big tough guy whose manliness is so great he was able to walk out on his wife and leave her with two twin boys to raise on her own, Louis and Leo. Nice touch soldier. Also, why when I see you do I instantly think of Hulk Hogan? It's a bad look, Vincent. Try and lose it."

"Have you got anything important to say or are you just gonna be a total twat for the whole conversation?" Lea said.

DC laughed. "Let's not be throwing insults around lightly, Agent Donovan. It's not wise to insult the man who holds all the cards."

"I didn't even know we were playing a card game," Lea said.

"Oh, we're playing something a lot more serious than a card game, Lea. The stakes couldn't be any higher on this one."

"How about you stop flapping your mouth for a second and get on with this riddle, then?"

He laughed again then he began to speak. "Very well. Listen carefully because I'll only say this once. Here is your riddle: I speak without a mouth and hear without ears, I have no body, but I come alive with the wind. What am I?"

"I give up," Lea said.

"You disappoint me," said DC. "The answer is I am an echo. Just like you're ECHO, aren't you? I thought that was funny."

Lea was losing patience. "Why have you called me Claremont?"

"Please, call me DC."

"I'm hanging up."

"I don't advise it. You're going to want to hear what I have to say because I have a little surprise for you, that's why. I guess you're pretty busy right now trying to track me and the rest of my crew, in some desperate bid to get old Professor Haggblom back and get your hands on the mighty Crucible. Am I guessing right? Am I doing good? But the thing is, I know you guys are not to be messed with. That's how I was able to get Haggblom in the first place – because I'm able to read my enemy and look ahead. I knew who was bringing Haggblom over to Gotham today, so I did my homework. I knew what it would take to get one over on you. That's like how I know you're gonna track me down pretty soon wherever I hide, so I thought I'd have some fun and give you something else to do. Just to slow your asses down."

"What are you talking about?" Lea asked.

Hawke saw she was trying to keep her voice level and measured as she was talking to him, but he knew her well enough to tell she was beginning to grow apprehensive about whatever Claremont was alluding to.

"Take a guess," DC said.

"I'm not playing games, Claremont."

"But I like games. Don't disappoint me, Lea – you don't wanna disappoint me. The truth is, I might not stick to my promise about giving Haggblom back if you don't get me my money, get that pathetic asshole out of the White House and release Al-Hazari. Truth is, I might just blow a hole through Haggblom's head whenever I damn well feel like it. Do you know why I can do that? I can do that because I have the fucking Crucible."

Lea took a breath. "Okay. What did you mean when you said you were doing something to slow us down?"

Hawke and the others stepped closer, listening attentively to whatever answer was about to come, but making sure to stay off-camera. No sense in giving Claremont more information than was strictly necessary.

"Oh, that's easy," Claremont said with a cold chuckle. "We have your little friends, Kahlia and Ravi and you're going to do whatever the fuck I want, or they're both going to be deep-sixed by my good hand. I guess that's going to give you something to think about so now I'm going to say goodbye. I'll be in touch sooner than you think."

CHAPTER THIRTEEN

Hawke could barely believe what he had just heard. Problems were crashing down on him like waves on a shore of the most violent sea imaginable, one after the next without cessation, and each one stopping him from getting back up and making things right. First, they learnt the Crucible was something much more sinister than they had initially been led to believe, then Haggblom was violently snatched from them, along with his briefcase. Now, the Cayman Crew were claiming they had also kidnapped two of his team members.

He had little trouble accepting what he had just heard as the truth because a second later Lea held up her phone to show a photograph of each of the kidnapped teammates. There were two separate pictures, one of Kahlia and one of Ravi. Whether they were taken in the same place or not was impossible to tell, but they had both been badly beaten and were covered in cuts and bruises. They were both also gagged with a short strip of duct tape.

Hawke presumed they'd also been wearing a blindfold until the moment of the photograph when they had been removed to allow an identification of them.

This changed everything. Hawke made a circuit of the room, deep in thought as he worked through the problem, desperate for a solution to pull everything together. They had been hit and hit hard and their reaction had to be fast and effective. Within the space of sixty minutes, they had been subject to a brutal attack in the kidnapping of Haggblom, an outrageous ransom demand and finally the stomach-churning news that two of their own had been kidnapped by the Cayman Crew.

"We're gonna need some help," Lea said, knocking him from his thoughts.

"Right," Hawke said. "Alex, what about your contacts in the CIA?"

"Already on it," Alex said. "I made contact with some of my best friends from the agency while Claremont was talking. I'll let you know when they get back to me, but I've got to say right now – just being honest with you all – the CIA is a big beast and it moves slowly. Not only that but while we have some good friends there, we've also made our fair share of enemies over the past few years.

We can't rely on a constant supply of accurate dependable information and help from the agency. We need to be prepared to do this on our own."

"Would be faster working on our own anyway," Scarlet said.

Hawke felt like he was at the foot of an unclimbable mountain, fighting back a deep rage he had not felt so strongly since the murder of Lexi back in the Congo. He found himself drowning in questions, but answers were in short supply. He fought it all back and tried to climb on top of the problem, to straighten his thoughts.

"I hate to be the one to say it," he said, "but we're going to need proof-of-life of Ravi and Kahlia before anything else happens. Those pictures could have been taken hours ago. They could both be dead by now. He must know that!"

As if DC had read Hawke's mind, another call arrived on Lea's phone.

"Looks like another call," she said, hitting play and holding it up for the others to see.

DC's voice began to speak. "I guessed you wouldn't accept the photographic images of your two colleagues as evidence that they were still alive, so we were prepared to make this little call. Enjoy."

As he spoke, the camera now swung around from his face to Kahlia and Ravi, who were both sitting where they had been for the photographs. They were still gagged and this time they were blindfolded too.

DC continued. "As pleased as you must be to see that your two colleagues are both alive and kicking, unfortunately, it's not all good news. Each one of your friends is wearing a little backpack, as you will now see, and in each backpack, there are enough plastic explosives to give them a one-way trip to the moon."

The camera now moved around behind Kahlia and Ravi to reveal both of them were wearing backpacks as DC had just explained. A black gloved hand appeared in the frame, reaching forward to the backpack on Kahlia's back. It opened the backpack to reveal what was, at least from a visual inspection over the video, an enormous quantity of plastic explosives. It then revealed something even more terrifying, a timer fixed to the top of the plastic explosives. At the moment it was not running.

DC went on. "The more astute among you will have noticed that these plastic explosives are attached to a timing device. And guess what?"

The gloved hand leaned forward and flicked a switch on the timer. It instantly flashed to life to reveal a series of red digits set at six hours.

The gloved hand pushed the button and the countdown immediately began ticking down. Hawke watched in horror as the tenths of a second whirled invisibly in a blur beside the full seconds which were already counting down on their way to the first minute.

"Oops – look what we went and did," DC said. "Now you'll see that you've got a little bit less than six hours to save your two friends. Because believe me, when the shit in these backpacks goes up you're gonna need a mop and bucket to take your friends back to your little island for their burial. The problem you've got is that New York City is a big fucking place and your little friends could be anywhere in the entire metropolitan area. But then again, am I lying? Perhaps your friends are in Rio de Janeiro? Perhaps your friends are in Alaska. I'm just kidding. They're right here in Gotham, where all the action takes place."

Hawke watched as the gloved hand closed up Kahlia's backpack and then opened Ravi's to show a similar setup. The gloved finger now activated the timer in Ravi's backpack. Hawke felt sick when the camera moved around to reveal the terrified faces of his blindfolded, gagged colleagues, sitting in absolute terror, on colossal quantities of the most dangerous explosives on Earth. He thought he saw a tear leaking from Kahlia's eye, but then she was blindfolded again, as was Ravi.

"You're gonna pay with your life for doing this to us," Hawke said. "You can count on that."

DC laughed. "Yeah, yeah, sure. I hear it all the time. I tell you what. Now you've had your fucking proof of life you can spend your time trying to find your little buddies before they get blown to pieces as well as sorting out my ransom demands. Oh, and by the way – here's a little hint – you might find a little surprise or two for you along the way. Ready, set, go ECHO!"

DC hung up.

Silence filled the hotel room. They had let their guard down and paid the price. They had allowed one of their charges to be snatched right from under them along with extremely sensitive research material, and now two of their teammates had also been kidnapped and were being held at gunpoint with explosives strapped to them. Hawke cursed himself for having been so sloppy and he saw from the others' faces that they felt the same way.

"Okay, here's what we do," Hawke said suddenly. "We're gonna split into two teams. Lea and Ryan, you're going to work with me. We're going track down this bloody Cayman Crew, or whoever's behind the snatching of Haggblom and the hacking of the Times Square billboard. We're going to take them out. While we're on that, Cairo will lead Reaper and Alex to locate and rescue Kahlia and Ravi. No one is going to die on this mission except members of the Cayman Crew, is that clear?"

A series of simultaneous nods showed Hawke everyone was clear, but no one spoke. Then, there was a knock at the door.

Hawke stared at the others and they stared back at him. No one spoke. The Englishman drew his Glock and walked over to the door. After looking through the spyhole and seeing nothing, he opened the door cautiously with his gun raised into the aim but found nothing other than a small box located on the floor, right in front of their door.

Hawke nudged the package with the toe of his boot. He was checking for weight and to see if anything was loose inside it. He heard something sliding around inside and calculated the weight at no more than a few ounces. He peered down both ends of the corridor on either side of the room to make sure that no one was there, then he stooped, picked up the box, stepped back inside the hotel room and closed the door.

"Someone has sent us a little gift," he said.

The others stayed quiet, standing around in a horseshoe shape in the hotel room, staring across at Hawke inside the entry vestibule by the door. He walked right through them and placed the box down on the bed. He then holstered the Glock and began to open the box, but Lea grabbed his arm and stopped him.

"What the hell do you think you're doing?" Lea said.

Hawke stopped and looked up into her eyes. "I'm opening the box," he said flatly. "Somebody's gone to the effort to send us this little gift and I want to know what it is."

"There could be anything in there! I know you're an Englishman, but surely you've thought of that?"

"Thanks for that," Hawke said, shaking his head to dismiss her concerns, he went back to opening the box. As he ran his thumb onto the duct tape he said, "If they wanted us dead, they wouldn't be titting around with something like this. They're communicating with us. You have to have both parties alive if you want to communicate."

He pulled out the smartphone.

"See? I was right! They want to communicate with us."

Lea looked sceptical. "They just did that when they called me!"

The phone trilled gently.

Without fear, Hawke took the call.

"Hello again," a voice said. "It's me again, your friendly host DC. Only this time, I'm sorry to tell you this is just a recording of my voice. I know that that will make you all very sad. Here's the thing – after our recent conversation about your two unfortunate teammates, I decided to give you a break, but to take advantage of my kind offer, you're gonna have to use your noggins. Riddle me this: to find your friends you must ask the angel who troubles the water. Good luck, team!"

"It's another bloody riddle," Scarlet said, kicking the end of the bed.

"It's from the Bible," Lea said immediately. "John 5:2-9. It's about healing waters at a pool in Jerusalem – the angel troubles them – but we'd probably say 'stir' today."

"What good is that to us?" Reaper asked. "Is there somewhere in New York called Jerusalem?"

Alex shook her head. "There's nowhere specifically called Jerusalem in the city."

"But in the Bible, the pool's location was more specific than just Jerusalem," Lea said. "It was in Bethesda."

Alex's eyes lit up with hope. "Bethesda Terrace and Fountain in Central Park! It's totally iconic! It's gotta be that they're talking about – specifically the statue there – the Angel of the Waters!"

Hawke's attention was snapped back to the phone in his hand by the sound of manic laughter. He looked down onto the screen to see the face of a court jester laughing and a short repeated gif of five seconds. Beneath it was a twenty-second countdown. His blood turned to ice in his veins.

"We have to get out of here now!"

"You think it's gonna blow?" Ryan said.

"Yeah, I think it's gonna blow!"

"Well, we can't just leave it here!" Lea said. "We don't know how powerful it is. This is a hotel, for god's sake. There are innocent people everywhere."

"And we can't throw it out the window or take it with us," Hawke said. "We have to go and we go now! There's only ten seconds left!"

Hawke ran into the bathroom and flushed the phone down the toilet, then he burst back into the room to find everyone else filing out through the main door. He joined them and then sprinted down the corridor, banging on the doors of their neighbours as they went and screaming at them to get out of their rooms. With a handful of confused civilians dragging along behind them, they reached the far end of the corridor.

Hawke was reasonably satisfied he had done all he could do to contain any damage or injury to other people. Then an almighty explosion detonated in their hotel room, shaking the entire floor and sending a thick noxious cloud of grey smoke mixed with plaster and wood chips and dirt and dust rolling towards them at speed down the corridor.

"Everyone out!" Hawke yelled. "The blast might have caused structural damage!"

"And what a great start to the mission," Scarlet said as they headed for a fire escape leading to some stairs. "These bastards have been a step ahead of us all along."

Reaper kicked open the fire door. "And something tells me this is only going to get worse."

CHAPTER FOURTEEN

Hawke led the team down the stairs and kicked open a panic bar on the ground floor before streaming out of the hotel into an alleyway around the back. The snowy air was already full of the sound of emergency sirens, this time racing towards the hotel in response to the explosion moments ago in their room.

"It's not gonna take them long to know that it went off in our room," Lea said.

"Whose name did we book the hotel under?" Ryan asked.

Alex half-raised her hand. "Mine."

"I don't see what difference it makes," Scarlet said. "Getting in and out of that place, we'd have been under more camera surveillance than an X-Factor contestant."

"Cairo's right," Ryan said. "Any authorities that want to find out who was renting the room at the time of the explosion will probably already have our faces and they'd have used facial recognition to identify us."

"It makes no difference," Lea said, stepping into the conversation. "We can't risk being captured by the authorities while we have this mission underway, so let's split up and keep moving."

Hawke couldn't have agreed more. "I want to know how explosives that powerful could be inside a regular phone. That's not right. Nothing I know of could do that."

"We can talk about it later," Lea said. "We should split up and get going."

The two teams split up, with Scarlet leading her team away to the south and Hawke leading Lea and Ryan down the alley at the back of the hotel before slowing to a stroll and stepping out onto the next street. Hawke told Ryan to start looking into the Cayman Crew in more detail while scanning the street for a couple of vehicles. Glancing down another alleyway, he saw an old 1980s Chevrolet.

"Perfect for the job," he said. "That's got exactly the level of security that I'm looking for."

Five minutes later, Hawke, Lea and Ryan had dumped their weapons in the boot and were cruising through Manhattan in the old Chevy, having successfully evaded any trouble back near the hotel following the explosion.

Ryan now leaned forward from the back seat and began reading off his telephone.

"I think I have something here, Joe," Ryan said. "Did some sniffing around and found an old article in the New York Post archive. A guy here was arrested for trafficking illegal weapons into the city nearly twenty years ago. He was given an eight-year sentence as he was playing a more peripheral role in someone else's gang. The leader of the gang was given twenty-five years and as far as I can tell he is still inside Sing Sing Prison. The good news is another little Herbert was helping them, called Tyler Cain. A sentence of five years and as far as I can tell from my devious little researches, he's still living in New York City, specifically South Jamaica in Queens, where he rents a small studio."

"What's the connection?" Lea asked.

"The gang was called The Cleaners."

"DC's old gang??"

"Give that woman a cigar."

"Thanks, Ryan. That's excellent news," Hawke said. "If you could be so kind as to provide the necessary navigation directions to Mr Cain, I should be only too glad to take us there forthwith."

Lea and Ryan exchanged an amused glance before Ryan punched the directions into the internet and quickly came up with the most efficient route to take them to Cain's address.

"All yours," he said.

"I believe it is," Hawke said. "Cain, I mean."

*

Kids wrapped up in hooded coats and scarves were playing an impromptu game of 21 outside the rowhouse where Tyler Cain's studio was located, bouncing a basketball and taking free shots, even in the snow. Hawke saw that as a potential problem if anything got tasty in the firearms department, but with so little time he had little choice but to ignore it. Offering them money to get lost might backfire in a big way and cause even more trouble, plus he was fairly certain he could handle an old lag from Sing Sing Prison without resorting to shooting irons.

Hawke instinctively reached round and felt for his Glock as they made their way down the slushy sidewalk, passing a downhill bodega and other brick and vinyl-siding buildings, as he closed in on Cain's address. At the end of the block, he heard the jangling clatter of an elevated J-Train, blending with the low grumbling beat of some drill music spilling out from a passing car. It was familiar; it was not his first time in this part of town. He walked up the steps of the rowhouse, located Tyler Cain's doorbell and pushed the buzzer. A moment later a tired, weak voice sounded through the crackly speaker.

"Who is it?"

Hawke paused a beat. "Courier."

"I didn't order anything. Get lost."

"It's a gift, man."

Cain sighed deeply and then the door clicked open. Two minutes later they had stepped inside, walked up to Cain's studio, and rung the doorbell. Hawke was now pressing the muzzle of his Glock up against Cain's forehead and pushing him back inside the apartment.

Cain was no pushover, having previously been a member of a bank robbery gang and mixed with the very worst New York society had to offer inside Sing Sing, so he took it in his stride and simply raised his hands, presuming this was just another robbery in what could be a fairly dangerous part of the city.

"You can see how much my watch is worth," Cain said calmly. "You want me to take it off? I'll take it off. The TV is a piece of junk and there's no cash in the house."

"I don't want your watch, your TV or any money," Hawke said calmly. "All I want from you is information."

Cain's brow furrowed as he took in what he had just heard. "Well, you don't need to be pressing that fucking gun into my head for information, man."

Hawke took the point, removed his finger from the trigger and pulled the gun away but kept it unholstered, hanging at his side just in case it was needed at a later date. He had no idea what was hidden around Tyler Cain's delightful studio apartment.

"We want to know where we can find a man called Franklin Claremont," Lea said. "People working for him usually call him DC."

Cain laughed. "Yeah, I know DC. Did some time with him back in the day. I heard he did a deal with the authorities that got him out sooner, at my expense too. I'd be happy to do anything to pay him back for that favour."

"I want to know where to find him," Hawke said flatly. "And I want to know now."

Cain shrugged. "Why?"

"You don't need to know why," Hawke said. "Just give me the address and we'll be out of your hair."

Tyler Cain pointed with both hands towards his desk which was pushed up against a wall on the side of the apartment under the window. Outside in the street, the sound of the basketball banging on the sidewalk had stopped. Things were quiet except for an occasional car cruising down the road outside.

"Old addresses are in a book on this desk. OK if I get it out?"

"Make sure that's all you get out," Hawke said, raising the gun back into the aim. "I'll squeeze this trigger before you get anything out of that drawer that I don't like the look of. Know it and believe it."

Cain took a moment, staring into Hawke's eyes. "Yeah, something tells me you really would."

Hawke watched Cain open the drawer and pull out an address book. He flicked through the pages before stopping around halfway through, where he tore out a page.

He handed Hawke the address. "This is where you need to go if you want to find DC, but if I were you, I'd forget about it right now."

"We don't have the luxury of forgetting about it, mate. Is that DC's address?"

Cain shook his head. "Nah, it's one of his old partners. One of the gang. Zeke. It's where Zeke Mercer lives. He's been there since he got shot."

"Shot?" Ryan asked.

"A personal thing."

"How dangerous is he?" Lea asked.

"Not as dangerous as DC, that's for damn sure, but you still wouldn't want to screw with him. We're talking about someone who spent twenty-five years in prison for armed robbery. He's knocked off more banks in Atlantic City than you've had hot dinners."

"He keeps firearms, I take it," Hawke asked.

Cain stood up and walked over to his refrigerator.

"Careful what you pull out of there, Cain," Hawke said, aiming the Glock at Cain's temple.

"I sure will, man."

Cain swung open the door and when he closed it again he was holding an ice-cold bottle of beer. He placed the cap down on the edge of the countertop and smacked it with the palm of his hand, breaking the cap off and producing a gentle hissing sound. As the spinning cap slowed to a stop on the countertop, he lifted the bottle to his lips and took several long gulps of the refreshing liquid. When he finished, he smacked his lips and belched and then fixed his eyes on Hawke.

"To say Zeke Mercer keeps guns is somewhat of an understatement. Just off the top of my head, I would say that Zeke Mercer probably possesses more guns than most small European nations, and not only that, he knows how to use them too. He wouldn't think twice about putting a bullet through any one of your heads."

"What is this address?" Lea asked. "An apartment?"

Cain shook his head. "Nah. He runs a business – a locksmith. That's what he did for the bank robbery gang back in the day. It's in Hunts Point in the Bronx. It's on Viele and Bryant. And don't screw around in that part of the city either because it's one of the most dangerous places that the Big Apple has to offer."

"What does he look like?" Hawke asked.

Cain gave a lengthy description of Mercer and then belched loudly.

"Thanks," Hawke said. "You've been most helpful."

"It's cool, dude."

THE MIDNIGHT SYNDICATE

Hawke, Lea and Ryan left the apartment. Hawke turned to the others and said: "Time for a chat with Zeke."

CHAPTER FIFTEEN

The Witch Doctor had been standing for hours, simply staring into the large, broken mirror fixed shoddily to the back of his apartment door. His body was nothing to write home about. In his late forties, he was eighty pounds overweight with fat hanging off him in all the usual places. He was severely out of shape and found climbing out of a chair a genuinely difficult challenge. His face was battered and weathered by a lifetime of physical abuse which came in the form of heavy alcohol consumption and smoking drugs, and he hadn't shaved for weeks, allowing him to see that most of his beard had now turned a grimy grey colour. He viewed the world through a pair of thick, black-framed spectacles.

Most of his condition, he knew, was because of a sedentary life, spent sitting in a chair working his voodoo, casting his magic spells on poor unsuspecting victims using the strange magical tools at his disposal, tools he had spent a lifetime learning how to master. His body and his face reeked of neglect, and large soft bags under his eyes, the colour of ripe avocados, reflected his terrible sleep habits, which sometimes amounted to no more than three or four hours on a good night. He'd tried to burn some of it off on a Peloton but to no avail. No amount of exercise, or even Spellwork was going to turn back the clock for this guy.

His eyes danced over his bloated stomach and the chubby rolls of fat around his chin and jowls, across the dirty-looking stubble and over the big bags beneath his eyes before finally settling on the eyes themselves. Now a smile appeared on the Witch Doctor's face. The eyes reflected the one part of him that was sharper than anyone else. His genius, a true brilliance that was the essence of him, punctuating his sad, tired battered face like two diamonds in a pile of horse excrement. These eyes were the gateways to the sanctuary of his mind, the place where the magic was born. His mind, somewhere he had spent almost his entire life living – and never in the outside world – was the portal to the deep black magic that he enjoyed inflicting on other people so much. This was where the voodoo happened. It was only when he took a moment out like this and looked into his eyes, that he was able to see his true self and now he once again refreshed his confidence in himself.

This was good because the Director was not known to take prisoners. The truth was that the Witch Doctor lived in fear of the Director even though the Director had promised the Witch Doctor the world. The Director had made certain that the Witch Doctor saw him execute the last man who disappointed him, and the Witch Doctor knew why – it was a warning, a lesson that he would never forget. Do not disappoint the Director. The Witch Doctor was confident there would be no disappointment. He was the greatest worker of black magic the world had ever seen, with the right tools he could use his magic to target anyone, to disrupt, to break, to hurt, to cause havoc, to destroy and even to kill.

He knew the Director would not be disappointed.

He turned away from the mirror and waddled over to his desk, upon which were carefully arranged the sacred objects he needed to conduct his spells. He stared at them in awe, knowing more than anyone else in the world the mighty power of which they were capable. Then he sat down in his chair, feeling the rolls of fat around his body come to a gentle and grateful rest on top of his thighs and set to work.

CHAPTER SIXTEEN

Tyler Cain had not been kidding when he said that Mercer's Locksmith Services was in a tough part of town. Hawke had visited some dangerous urban places in the past and he knew as soon as he drove into Hunt's Point, that this was one of those places. He had certainly seen a lot worse, but there was deprivation and decay in abundance. Walls were graffitied, the gutters were full of trash, heavy industrial-strength roller blinds covered most of the doors and windows and there were more than the average number of broken car wrecks parked up on the side of the road with smashed windows and slashed tyres.

"Not exactly on the tourist trail, is it?" Lea said.

They cruised past a junkyard and pulled up at the address Cain had given to them. Hawke climbed out of the car and slammed his door shut. Lea and Ryan joined him. The sky was still grey but the snowing had stopped, at least for now. At the sides of the road, thick piles of black snow were heaped up where a snowblower had dumped them. His breath condensed in the air as he rubbed his hands and reached around to check his Glock was where it should be.

The junkyard was over to their right and seemed to be harbouring more than old car wrecks. A gaggle of men in sherpa-lined fleece jackets and baseball caps were just visible through the open front gates, and they looked like they were doing anything but trading in scrap metal. Ahead of him was Mercer's Locksmith Services. All the men except one turned and climbed into vehicles, driving away from the junkyard and leaving Mercer on his own.

"What do you say we give the old bastard a call?" Hawke said.

Lea checked her weapon and nodded her head. "Sounds like a plan to me, Joe."

The three of them walked away from the car, crossed the sidewalk and made their way up the paved path leading to the locksmith shop. Hawke went first, pushing open the door and stepping inside a small, grotty reception area. The floor was stained vinyl and the walls were fake pine beadboard plastered with old calendars. A speed-painted acrylic picture of a tropical beach sunset was the centrepiece, hanging at an odd angle above the calendars. The heating was cranked up to full.

A man came out. Hawke recognised him as the man from the car park. Mercer.

Mercer was in his fifties but still fit and lean. The sherpa was gone to reveal a wife beater and ripped muscles covered in tattoos, including one Hawke recognised instantly – a skull wearing a Delta Force beret. The wife-beater was stained with oil and grease and maybe what looked something like egg yolk. Downstairs, he was wearing a pair of old blue jeans held up with a scuffed black leather belt. He wore no jewellery of any kind and he wore no watch. His face was a TV screen, showing a nonstop movie of hardship, fights and deprivation. When he looked into Hawke's eyes, he was immediately suspicious.

"Can I help?"

"I think maybe you can," Hawke said.

"I think maybe I can too," Mercer said, "but I'm guessing this ain't got much to do with locks."

The atmosphere thickened, and Mercer's eyes crawled from Hawke to Lea across to Ryan and back to Hawke again.

"I wouldn't say that," Hawke said, in his usual cheery English accent. "We need you to unlock something for us. And we heard that you're just a man to do it."

"Unlock what?" Mercer asked humourlessly.

"Well, that's just it," Lea said, stepping into the conversation for the first time. "We don't need you to unlock a lock *per se*, we need you to unlock a little mystery for us. You see, we flew into New York City this morning to do a job and what do you know, everything goes shit-shaped. Just like that. The next thing you know, we're having a conversation with Tyler Cain, but he pointed us in your direction."

Mercer looked away, and Hawke watched his eyes crawling in the space under the counter in between them. Now Mercer returned his gaze to the visitors in his shop.

"I don't know anybody called Tyler Cain."

"That's funny because he knows you," Ryan said. "He gave us a perfect description down to your tattoo and that delightful apparel you're sporting this morning."

Mercer's expression changed. Hawke watched his eyes once again crawling around in the area beneath the counter. Now he looked back up at them again, specifically at Ryan.

"That ain't polite."

"We're looking for DC," Lea said, smiling at him. "If that helps clear things up."

"And I don't know no DC neither," Mercer said.

Lea walked to the counter getting in between Hawke and Mercer and standing on tiptoes to make her eyes reach Mercer's level. Hawke knew what she was doing – blocking Mercer's line of sight and giving Hawke a chance to reach for his weapon.

"I don't believe you," Lea said. "I think that not only do you know DC, but that you worked with him on a lot of bank jobs over the years in Atlantic City. Not only this, but I think that you can tell us exactly where to find him this morning, which would be good for us because he's the reason everything went shit-shaped for us."

Mercer looked away, looking down under the counter one more time. Without warning, he reached beneath the counter and then slipped out of sight for a second. Hawke had already drawn his Glock and now Lea stepped to his left and drew hers. Over on the right side of the counter, Ryan was also reaching for his weapon, but by now Mercer had reappeared again, rolling away from the counter and coming to a stop, sitting on his backside with his back up against the back wall. Hawke and Lea saw the problem first, then Ryan a second later. The problem was that Mercer was now holding a Remington pump action shotgun and was aiming it at Hawke.

Then he fired.

CHAPTER SEVENTEEN

When the Remington exploded in the small office, Hawke was already on the floor. The shot went everywhere, with dozens of pieces of lead embedding in the ceiling tiles and some of them smashing the large glass door behind them.

Then chaos ensued in the tiny office.

Lea had the best angle and was first to fire back, firing three shots at Mercer. The first two missed and the third one tore into his calf. She had aimed low on purpose because he still had questions to answer, but now the New York locksmith and former bank robber took the round like a man, barely offering a grunt in pain before operating the composite slide on the pump action shotgun, which acted as the bolt system, and letting rip a second time, this time in Lea's direction.

Like Hawke, her many years fighting with ECHO had given her a kind of sixth sense and in this case, it wasn't difficult to work out what happened when you fired three shots at a man with a pump-action shotgun and struck him in the leg with one of them. She knew what happened next, and she was on the floor by the time Mercer had squeezed the trigger. This time the shot peppered the wall behind her, shattering the tropical beach picture and blasting it off the wall.

Both Hawke and Ryan were on their feet, aiming their weapons at Mercer, but now he rolled out of the office through a side door and was clean out of sight, leaving nothing but a cloud of gun smoke and chaos behind him.

Hawke looked at Lea. "You OK?"

She nodded. "Sure, I'm okay. What about you?"

"I'll be OK when we know where DC is. Let's go."

"Hey! I am also OK," Ryan said. "Thanks for asking. You know how to make a guy feel loved and valued."

With the Glock still in his left hand, Hawke ran to the counter, planted his right hand on the top of it and bolted over the top. Ryan rolled his eyes, raised the hinged flip-up countertop, and casually strolled through with Lea behind him.

"What can I say?" Hawke said, having watched them walk through. "It was much more fun to vault over the thing."

They burst through the door to find themselves in a large workshop full of locksmith's equipment bolted down to greasy chisel-marked benches. Hawke had already seen Mercer slipping into the shadows behind one of the key-cutting machines. He thought about firing but knew better than wasting a round on someone just to send them a signal, at least in a situation like this. Mercer already knew all of the signals. He led the others forward slowly, their guns raised into the aim and was struck by the strong smell of lock lubricants and metal filings hanging heavily in the workshop air.

He heard shuffling. Mercer was crawling to a new location on his hands and knees, but being careful to keep out of sight behind a line of workbenches at the far end of the shop. In his new position, Mercer popped up and fired on them, his aim was good, but not good enough, and went off to their left, not even driving them to the floor. In response, all three of them opened fire on him, but he was too fast. He also knew what came next after firing on three people armed with Glocks. Their bullets were on target, but the only problem was the target wasn't there anymore so now they were wasted peppering holes in a box full of tension wrenches and key blanks on the bench behind where Mercer had been.

Hawke heard shuffling again, then the familiar *cha-chunk* sound of Mercer operating the Remington's pump handle to cycle the bolt, chambering a new cartridge and automatically ejecting the previous one, which Hawke now heard hitting the concrete floor and rolling to a stop somewhere. Mercer appeared in an entirely new location three metres to the right of where he had previously been. Then he vanished again.

"Damn it, Joe! This is like a game of bloody Whac-A-Mole!" Lea said.

"Over there!" Ryan yelled, pointing.

Hawke followed Ryan's pointing finger and saw Mercer leap from his new cover position and make a break for a closed fire door at the far left of the workshop. As Mercer kicked out with his boot at the panic bar to open the door, Hawke raised his gun and fired a shot into his other calf. It took only one bullet to finally stop Mercer in his tracks and now the former Delta Force soldier crashed forward into the fire door, headbutting the panic bar which opened the door, allowing him to tumble out into an alley at the back of his workshop.

Hawke and the others ran over to him. Lea booted the Remington out into the alley, while Hawke and Ryan grabbed an ankle each and dragged the man back into the workshop. Lea checked the alley was clear, and now Mercer was safely out of reach, she picked up the Remington and then returned to the workshop, closing the fire door gently behind her. By the time she laid the Remington down on one of the workbenches, Hawke and Ryan had lifted Mercer onto another one of the workbenches and were already going to work on him.

"I'll kill you for this, you bastards!" Mercer said.

Hawke looked at the two, shredded bleeding calves, and the blood soaking through into the shredded jeans on both of his legs and gave him a friendly smile. "You can't even walk mate. You're not gonna be doing any killing anytime soon."

"Yeah? You made a big mistake today, you stupid motherfuckers! You don't know who you're screwing with!"

Hawke was unfazed. He leaned in close to Mercer and lowered his voice. "Tell me where we can find DC."

"Get fucked."

"Thing is mate, right now I'm being polite," Hawke said. "I'm a polite guy and sometimes that slows things down a little bit for me. But the thing is today I can't let anything slow me down because a couple of very good friends of mine are in a spot of bother. Because the silage heap we both know as DC has a pile of plastic explosives strapped to them with a timer set on it and this gives me… what now?" Hawke checked his watch. "A little over five hours to try and find them. And if I fail in that task they both get blown to bits and I simply can't let that happen. So I'll ask one more time where do I find DC?"

"And I said get fucked."

"This is a very handy place to be, mate," Hawke said. "We have drill bits, bolt cutters, files, pliers, you name it. So many ways to make you talk."

"You ain't got the balls for it."

"Ryan – would you get me that blowtorch over there please?"

For the first time, Mercer looked nervous. He raised his head off the bench where he had been resting it and stared down his body for a moment, taking in the bleeding legs and the mess and the blood pooling on the workbench surface. Then he turned to look at the three people who had put him there and his demeanour changed.

"Listen, maybe we can do a deal."

"No, I don't think so," Hawke said. "You'll forgive me for saying so, but something tells me you're not the kind of person that I could strike a deal with. Call me crazy, but I think you might renege on it."

"Seriously man!" Mercer said, panic audible in his voice. "I can tell you where DC is all right? It's true, I used to work with DC – we did a lot of jobs together in Atlantic City back in the day, but look around man! I'm straight now – everything here is legit. I work my ass off man, going out in all weathers fixing locks. This is a legit business. I left DC behind a long time ago."

Hawke sighed. "Get me something to light the blowtorch with, Ryan."

"All right, all right!" Mercer said. "It's true that I left DC behind me a long time ago, and it's true that I run a legit business now, but I can still tell you how to get to DC. You guys have played a good game and there's more of you than me and you got the better of me and I'm man enough to put my hands up and surrender. There ain't no need for the fire stick man."

Ryan handed Hawke a handheld propane torch. "You don't need anything to light it, Joe – it's got a built-in igniter."

"Excellent work, Ryan," Hawke said, opening the valve on the small propane tank and turning the torch's gas control dial to a medium flame size. He turned back to Mercer on the bench. "I want to know where DC is and I want to know before this minute is up."

As he spoke, Hawke clicked the built-in igniter and lit the torch. The flame roared and hissed in a dazzling blue, orange and red flame.

"OK, man! Here's where you find DC – you gonna write this down or what?"

"I think we can manage to remember it between the three of us," Lea said. "Just get on with it before you get toasted on both sides."

Mercer's wide eyes stared at the torch in Hawke's hands. "So, DC has something to do with a place called Shangri La. I think that's maybe where the Cayman Crew are based. at least while they're here in New York City."

"How many people are in the Cayman Crew?" Lea asked.

"Not many," Mercer said. "And I don't even know all of their names. I only know what DC told me a few months back. The first thing you need to know is that a few weeks ago a guy named the Director got in touch with DC and told him that he had a big job and he needed their services. DC ain't exactly bothered by ethics or morality or nothing like that so he was only too happy to snap up the job for what this Director dude was willing to pay. Big bucks, man."

"How many people are in DC's crew?" Hawke asked, repeating Lea's question.

"It changes depending on the time of year. People come, people go. Sometimes they get shot, sometimes they leave – maybe if they upset DC they might go for a permanent swim, usually in the East River. Right now there's maybe six, seven or eight people in the crew."

"So, somewhere around maybe ten people including this Director?" Lea asked.

"No, that's not right. You don't get it. The Director ain't in the Cayman Crew. The Director is some other dude. DC said he was running something called the Midnight Syndicate."

Hawke, Lea and Ryan exchanged glances. This was a new one for all three of them and meant another layer of scum to break up and destroy.

"What is the Midnight Syndicate, Mercer?" Lea asked.

"Please don't ask me that because I ain't got a clue. Everything DC told me about them I just told you. I swear to God, man."

"I believe you," Hawke said. "So, you're telling us this Director runs something called the Midnight Syndicate, and it was that guy who hired DC and the Cayman Crew to do this latest job?"

Mercer nodded. "I think I need a hospital."

"And you're saying there's maybe eight people in the Cayman Crew?" Hawke asked, ignoring his pleas.

"Yeah, maybe something like that," Mercer said, lowering his head and letting it rest back down on the bench with a sigh. "And don't forget the Witch Doctor."

"Who the hell is the Witch Doctor?" Lea asked.

"I don't know much about him, neither," Mercer said. "I don't know anything about him at all. All DC told me was that his crew was hired by a dude called the Director to do a job for him and that there was this weirdo who hangs around the Director sometimes called the Witch

Doctor. He's part of the Midnight Syndicate. That is the honest-to-God whole truth."

"We'll see about that," Lea said

"I swear it man!"

"You're doing really well, Zeke," Hawke said with a grim smile. "Now we need to know where Shangri La is."

"I don't know," Mercer said, his voice once again becoming desperate. "But I swear I've told you everything I know. I've given you everything, even the name of the place… but DC never told me where Shangri La is."

Hawke brought the torch closer to the wounded man's legs. "I'll start down here on the legs Zeke, and I'll move my way up slowly. That way the pain gets progressively worse over time, and I'll make this go slower than a fucking chair lift."

"Damn it, man! I'm telling you the truth! You're a soldier, right? I know you're a soldier, so don't bother telling me that you're not. We're brothers man. You've gotta be Special Forces – I saw the way you moved back there in the office and what you're doing in here. You're British Special Forces, right? You're SAS, right?"

"How dare you!" Hawke said. "Take that back".

Lea rolled her eyes. "He was in the SBS. They're like the SAS but they play with boats a little bit more."

Mercer gave Lea a sly look. "I was in the Delta Force. I know what the SBS are and what they can do. Listen, man," he said turning to Hawke, "we're both cut from the same cloth – you know we are. Sure, I fell on some hard times after I came out of the army and I wound up working for DC. I regret some of that but you can see what I've done since I left his crew. I set up this business and it's legit, just like I said. I'm telling you the truth. You can put that flame all over me, but I'm never going to be able to tell you where Shangri La is. DC did talk to me a lot about an abandoned warehouse he was using on and off, somewhere in the city – maybe that's it – but I don't know where that is either. I swear it. We're brothers."

Hawke switched the torch off.

"I believe you," he said, "but you must know someone who can lead us to Shangri La. Someone from DC's past… someone DC might have told – anything."

"Maybe there's someone," Mercer said.

"Let's hear it then," Lea said, "before he turns that blowtorch back on."

"I think you're gonna like this, what with you being SBS and everything. There's a guy on DC's crew called Cambridge. A Brit. I think he was in the SAS. You might know him."

Hawke shook his head. "Never knew anyone with that name in the UK Special Forces, not while I was serving in them, anyway."

"No you don't understand – Cambridge isn't his name, it's where he was born. Everyone in DC's crew just uses their hometown as a codename. So DC was born in Washington, Cambridge was born in Cambridge, England and so on. You get it, right?"

Lea sighed. "Yeah, I think we get it."

"So this guy was in the SAS," Mercer continued, "but the thing is, he's got very loose lips after drinking."

"Where does he drink?" Hawke asked immediately.

"At a bar called O'Grady's in Brooklyn. Maybe he's blabbed to someone in there. That is honestly all I can think of, man."

Hawke threw the blowtorch into the corner of the room and signalled for the others to follow him out. He kicked open the fire door with his boot on the panic bar and turned back to Mercer.

"Thanks, Zeke," Hawke said. "And by the way, we're nothing like brothers."

CHAPTER EIGHTEEN

A cold north squall was blowing another wave of snow across Central Park as Scarlet, Reaper and Alex drove in a cab up Central Park West and then turned right into the park on West 72nd Street. The cab continued into the park, cruising past Strawberry Fields, the memorial to John Lennon, situated where it was because it was almost opposite The Dakota, the building outside which he had been murdered. Alex, a longtime Beatles fan, noted the memorial but her attention was soon drawn back to the moment when she heard Scarlet checking her weapon over and smacking the mag back into her grip. This solicited a strange look from the cab driver, but Scarlet told him she was British Secret Service and the accent seemed to do the trick. Then again, Alex thought, he was probably better armed than she was knowing a lot of New York cabbies.

They cruised past Cherry Hill, a Victorian-era water fountain then the cab driver finally pulled up at their final destination – the Bethesda fountain. The prominent feature was in some ways the centrepiece of the southern half of Central Park, famous for its ornate detail and neoclassical grandeur. They paid the driver and emerged into the cold, blustery day. A short walk through light snow brought them to the famous Angel of the Water statue, a female angel standing on a tiered pedestal with her wings stretched out behind her, cast in bronze. Opposite the statue, to the south, was the famous Bethesda Terrace, a large raised terrace covered in impressive decorative balustrades which provided tourists and other visitors to the park with a raised platform from which to enjoy the fountain surrounding the Angel of the Water statue below.

Alex stared up at the statue, scouring every inch of it for anything unusual. The riddle that the Cayman Crew had left on the smartphone back in the hotel room specified not only Bethesda but specifically referenced the Angel of the Waters. That narrowed things down a lot because searching the Bethesda Terrace for an unknown object was not something any of them would enjoy. Her thoughts were interrupted by Reaper who now cried out that he had found something, and at the same time, pointed up at the statue. He was standing on the opposite side of the central fountain pool from Alex and now Scarlet ran around to his position. Alex also made her way around, but by the time she got there, Reaper had already climbed into the fountain pool and was sloshing through the water past the lilies towards the statue.

Alex watched as the hardened Frenchman and former French Foreign Legionnaire now manhandled his way up the side of the statue until he was hanging off the side of it, almost looking as if he was dancing with the angel for a few seconds, but then he reached forward and tried to grab what he had seen. He fumbled with it for a few seconds and then reached into his pocket. A second later, he produced a pocket knife, which he manipulated and opened the blade before hacking away at something and then finally waving a mobile phone in the air. Then he pocketed the knife and sloshed back through the pool, joining the two women who were waiting for him on dry land.

"It's a cell phone! It was taped to the top of one of the angel's wings with duct tape!"

"Good work Vincent," Scarlet said, standing on tiptoes and kissing him on his unshaven cheek.

"Thank you, but the name is Reaper when I am on a mission."

He said this with a wry smile and then handed her the telephone.

"You'll be on a bloody mission in a minute," Scarlet said returning his smile. "A mission to find your balls, you silly sod."

Scarlet held the phone in her hand and noticed a slight trembling which was unusual for her, but having seen what happened to the first telephone back in the hotel room, she had serious misgivings about it happening again – especially if DC considered it funny to reduce the length of time in between the riddle and the explosion. For now, she had no choice other than to switch the phone on.

"It's another video," she said. "Listen up."

When the message started playing, Scarlet frantically clicked the volume control and turned it up as loud as it would go. She was almost certainly holding a palm full of explosives, just as had been the case with the mobile phone back in the hotel room, but as Hawke had said, these guys wanted to communicate the message, so for now she thought she was safe.

Then the message began to play. Reaper and Alex gathered around her to block noise and hear DC's next recorded message. As before, his voice was calm and icy cold: "I can't say that I am not disappointed that you're still here in the land of the living. I was kind of hoping you might have been blown to bits by my little surprise back in your hotel room. Nevertheless, if you found this phone and you're listening to this message then here you are, looking for the next riddle. Pay attention because here it is: 'Work as the great detective did and work for work's sake, because only by taking this line will you succeed'."

"I just Googled, it," Reaper said. "I'm getting a return for the words "work for work's sake" in a Sherlock Holmes story – The Adventure of the Priory School."

"That explains the reference to the great detective," Scarlet said. "What else did it say, Reap? Something about taking a line?"

Reaper read on through the paragraph in the section he had found. "Oui, it says that Sherlock Holmes takes 'a very high line in professional matters'. But does this help us?"

"The High Line!" Alex said, her heart pounding in her chest with the thrill of the chase. "It's a park built on an elevated railway line on the West Side! He must mean we have to go there!"

"Shit!" Scarlet said staring at the phone. She raised it so Reaper and Alex could both see the screen. Alex's heart pounded even faster when she saw the same jester's face that had appeared on the phone back in the hotel room, and the same twenty-second countdown.

"What the hell are we gonna do?" Alex asked frantically.

Scarlet was scanning the immediate area for somewhere she could throw the phone, but there were just too many people all over the place. It left her with no choice but to throw the phone into the fountain and scream at everyone to run as far away from it as they possibly could.

Alex sprinted alongside Reaper and Scarlet towards the tree line to the west of the fountain, barely reaching it when they heard the enormous explosion. She turned to see a giant fireball consuming the space where the fountain had once been. When the smoke finally cleared, she saw a bent and broken Angel of the Waters leaning over at a forty-five-degree angle and the wall surrounding the fountain completely broken. Water streamed out all over the terrace. Tourists and New Yorkers alike were screaming and running for their lives. Inevitable chaos ensued.

"Let's get the hell out of here," Scarlet said. "We need to stay one step ahead of the law and time is running out for us to find Ravi and Kahlia."

Alex never even looked back.

CHAPTER NINETEEN

Hawke's journey into Brooklyn was by cab. They made O'Grady's Bar in good time, paid the cab driver and walked a short distance along the snowy sidewalk before pushing open the entrance door and stepping inside. The atmosphere was the same as countless other Irish bars Hawke had visited over the years, with the bar bathed in the low amber glow of fairy lights and behind it several brightly flashing neon signs mostly in the form of beer and whiskey names – Budweiser, Guinness, Jameson.

Hawke continued over to the bar with Lea and Ryan right behind him. It was a rough no-nonsense place that had no doubt seen its fair share of bar brawls and broken noses, but there was a certain charm to the place with its antique décor and vintage Guinness Posters on the walls. An old, worse-for-wear Irish tricolour was pinned up on the far wall, demonstrating more than a hint of national pride, despite the thousands of miles distance between here and the motherland.

The old wooden floorboards creaked as Hawke made his way over to the barman. He continued to scan the bar as he went. The place was busy enough and a combination of loud laughter and likely banter added to a traditional Irish folk song playing on a 1960s jukebox in the corner, forcing Hawke to raise his voice as he spoke to the man behind the bar. He had already cased the entire bar for any sign of someone even vaguely reeking of the Regiment but seen no one that set off his radar.

The barman was midway through pouring a pint of Guinness and carefully judging the angle of the pint glass to ensure the perfect head on top of the stout when he looked up at Hawke and asked him what he wanted to drink. Enticed by the rich, peaty smell of the Guinness, Hawke was tempted to order a pint immediately, but remembering he was on a job, politely declined and instead went straight to the point.

"I'm trying to find someone."

"Then maybe try a dating website," said the barman, no smile.

"That's very good," Hawke said. "Let me try again. I'm looking for an old friend of mine who I know drinks in here from time to time."

"A lot of people drinking in here, buddy."

"Yeah, this guy he probably looks like he's in pretty good shape, in his fifties, and talks a bit like me."

The barman paused. "I think at least one guy fits the bill, but I'm not gonna tell you anything about him because for all I know you mean him harm."

Lea stepped forward and tried a different approach. "We don't mean him any harm," she said, her Galway accent immediately being noticed by several people drinking in the bar. "He's the one in danger and we're trying to help him."

The barman gave her a sceptical look. "And I'm supposed to just take your word for it, am I?"

She sighed and shrugged and ordered a single Jameson's whisky. Hawke noted she had slightly different views about drinking while on duty.

"We're not looking for any trouble," Lea continued, taking the whiskey and knocking it back in one, causing even more heads to turn and look at her. "We're just trying to help an old friend."

The barman relented. Finishing pouring the pint of Guinness, he walked over and handed it to a customer sitting at the far end of the bar. He took the money, ran it through the register and gave the man some change before walking back over to Hawke and the others. He spoke to Lea.

"Well, you look all right to me," he said. "Is that accent Mayo or Galway?"

"Galway," she said. "I'm from Connemara."

A smile finally broke through the man's large black beard. "I thought it was Connemara."

"No, you thought it was Mayo."

Hawke let them talk, sensing Lea was breaking through the ice.

"All right, I thought it was Mayo, but it's been a long time since I was in Ireland. It's where my parents came from originally. They came from Dublin."

Lea smiled. "So, you're gonna help me or not?"

"Look, the truth is the guy you're talking about is a bit of an asshole. All I can tell you is that he drinks in here whenever he's in town, but he's away a lot. He talks a lot of shit when he gets drunk about the 'missions' he's been on in the army. This asshole claims he was in the SAS. Give me a break."

"What's he call himself?" Lea asked.

The barman narrowed his eyes. "I thought you said he was a friend?"

"That might have been a slight exaggeration," Lea said. "But he's still in danger if we can't get to him."

"He calls himself Cambridge."

Hawke cursed inwardly and saw from the expressions on Lea's and Ryan's faces that they felt the same way. But then the barman said something else.

"But that's even more bullshit because I've seen his card when he pays off his tab. And the name on there ain't Cambridge. It's Michael Tanner."

"I could kiss you!" Lea said.

"OK." The barman pursed his lips and leaned forward over the bar.

"But I don't want to make everyone else in here jealous," she said with a wink. "Slán, Mr Barman."

"Huh?" The barman said.

"It means goodbye," Ryan said. "But I think she likes you."

CHAPTER TWENTY

Hawke watched Ryan stumble out of the 7-Eleven on the corner of the block and walk back over to their car, his arms bursting with grocery bags. Breath plumed from his mouth and steamed his glasses as he bumbled his way along the sidewalk back to their vehicle. Even with his preferred shaved head and tattoos, he would always be the same old nerd Hawke had first met back in London all those years ago.

"Sometimes he looks like a right berk," Hawke said. "I can't believe you married him."

"Yeah, although I *did* marry him... I still haven't married you yet," Lea said with a smile. "Maybe you should think about what that says."

Hawke went to reply but ran out of time as Ryan had reached the car, pulled open the back door handle and clambered into the rear of the vehicle, making it rock up and down on the suspension as he slammed the door. The interior of the car was instantly filled with the smell of hot grease and coffee.

"What the hell have you got in there?" Hawke asked. "It smells like a KFC grease trap."

"Mmmm," Ryan said. "Agreed."

Hawke stared at him. "I thought we were just getting coffee?"

"Yeah, I got everyone a coffee," Ryan said. "And a couple of snacks if that's ok. I haven't eaten anything since the plane into New York."

"So what's in there?" Lea said, leaning over the seat and peering inside one of the grocery bags.

"Just a couple of hot dogs knocked up on one of the roller grills in there," Ryan said. "And also some pizza slices, and some nachos with cheese and something called a Kizza."

"What the hell?" Lea asked.

"It's some kind of combination between a kebab and a pizza."

"Not for me, thanks." She looked disgusted. "Looks and smells like hot roadkill."

"So not just coffees then," Hawke said with a sigh.

"No, not just coffee," Ryan said, his head dipping into the bag as he rummaged around looking for various items. "I also got some trail mix, a packet of beef jerky and some hot pretzels. Want some?"

"Just the coffee will do fine, thank you," Hawke said. Looking in the mirror, he saw Ryan was already tearing his way into one of the packs of beef jerky.

Lea took her coffee and one of the hot pretzels and pressed back into her seat up front. Beside her, Hawke sipped his coffee. It tasted good, at least considering the circumstances and given Hawke's background in the Marines, and considering the kind of coffee he got served up there, especially while on operations, he couldn't be a coffee snob.

"Enjoying the jerky, Ryan?"

With his mouth still half full, and chomping away happily, Ryan nodded and began to speak through the beef. "Yeah, I love this stuff. For some reason, it always tastes different in London. Are you sure you're not hungry, Joe? At least try one of the pretzels. How about a slice of Kizza?"

Hawke shook his head and said no again. He was enjoying the coffee, plain and simple and people-watching outside the windscreen of the parked Chevy. He'd been staring at the intersection one hundred yards or so ahead of them, watching an endless stream of Japanese and American sedans, Ford Minivans, Teslas, Isuzu delivery trucks and Gillig buses trundling past each other on their way to various destinations. The car shook slightly as a Peterbilt garbage truck cruised close by them followed by an old Ford Crown Victoria taxicab, which you saw less and less these days, having been replaced by the Nissan MV 200, the official New York City taxi for ten years now. But Hawke liked the old stuff, so gave the tired old Ford an appreciative nod as it cruised by in the wake of the garbage truck.

"Maybe we need to think less about pretzels and more about Michael Tanner," he said at last with his eyes fixed on Ryan in the rearview mirror.

Ryan's reply was typically nonchalant. "Oh, I'm talking about pretzels because I already know all about Tanner."

Hawke and Lea exchanged a glance and then both leaned over their seats to stare at Ryan who was sitting behind them, his mouth now full of nachos and cheese.

"You already know about Michael Tanner?" Lea asked.

Ryan nodded.

"And when exactly were you going to share this information with us?" Hawke asked. "You might have noticed we're on a countdown to destruction here."

Ryan was fumbling for the phone in his pocket, and with his mouth still full of nachos and cheese and balancing a cup of coffee on his knee, he whipped the phone out and began to scroll through to his desired page.

"Michael Tanner," Ryan began. "First of all, he is a former SAS. So it might be worth asking Cairo if she knows anything about him. He was thrown out of the Regiment, dishonourably discharged, but very discreetly so as not to bring any shame on such a prestigious organisation…"

"Let's not get silly," Hawke said. Seeing the look on Lea's face he relented. "All right, it was just a little dig. Just a little professional rivalry. Some in-jokes, that's all."

"Carry on please, Ryan," Lea said.

"Yes, the full lowdown on Tanner would be helpful please", Hawke said sipping his coffee.

Ryan had now switched things up, so he was holding his coffee again and the phone was balancing on his knee as he read the information from the screen.

"Mike Tanner was born in England, in the Peak District, where he would be taken camping by his father out in the woods and hills of the region, and this is where he developed his interest in the great outdoors. He was born into a military family, his father was a regular infantryman in the Grenadier Guards. Tanner followed in his footsteps, joining the British Army at sixteen years old, going into the Grenadier Guards like his father, as a regular infantryman, having dropped out of school with barely any grades. He joined the SAS as a Trooper at twenty-four years old after eight years of service in the Guards. According to this he was very highly regarded by the Regiment, participating in several highly classified missions around the world, including work in Iraq, Afghanistan, and Sierra Leone."

"So, far so normal," Hawke said.

"Yeah, but this is where things get interesting," Ryan said. "Tanner's career took an unexpected turn during a mission somewhere. This is fully redacted even from his records – the details of this mission are classified by the looks of things, but there are references in his medical files to him being haunted by something that happened to him on this mission, and I think this is where the rot began. He began disobeying orders, especially those given by senior officers and was eventually dishonourably discharged and booted out into Civvy Street."

"I wonder what happened?" Lea asked.

"It's not important," Hawke said. "At least not at the moment. Anything else Ryan?"

"Not much," Ryan said after sipping his coffee. "After he rejoined society he quickly found himself on the wrong side of the law, and that was when he began working as a criminal in bank robbery gangs. After a certain amount of time, it looks like he ran into the man we know as DC and joined the Cayman Crew."

Lea finished her coffee. "Is there anything that can help us find him?"

"Yeah, there is. Thanks to some rather unorthodox hacking, I know he entered the United States on a fake passport, travelling as a man named Logan Reed. Three days later, a warehouse was hired out by a man named

Logan Reed. Now there's a chance it's a different Logan Reed, but right now it's all we've got."

"A warehouse?" Lea said. "Remember what Mercer said about DC talking about an abandoned warehouse? That has to be Shangri La!"

Hawke agreed. "That's gotta be our man. You know the exact location of this warehouse, right?"

Ryan finished his coffee and belched loudly before reaching into the bag and pulling out a packet of trail mix. "I sure do. You need to get this Chevy on the road and make a left at that intersection. After that, I'll give you lefts and rights because that's just the kind of guy I am."

Hawke smiled as he turned the ignition and fired the engine up.

Sensing Lea's eyes staring at him, he finally relented. "Good work, Ryan."

CHAPTER TWENTY-ONE

Vincent Reno liked to be called Reaper while on a mission, but these days he began to wonder if maybe he was growing out of his callsign. After all, the call sign 'Reaper' had been given to him many years ago – in the original French 'Le Faucheur' – back when he had joined the French Foreign Legion. He was still in his twenties. A drill sergeant in the Legion had once told him after a few drinks that a more capable and stronger man he had never met inside the ranks. His stamina had been unsurpassed, as had been his tolerance of hardship and deprivation. He had also excelled in demonstrating absolutely zero reluctance when it came to executing his orders and neutralising the enemy. It was the act of rapidly building up the largest body count of his entire battalion that had earned him his moniker.

The Reaper.

Vincent Reno nearly always thought in French, even when on a mission with his colleagues in ECHO, so he tended to see himself as 'Le Faucheur', but 'Reaper' was just as good to hear.

Until now.

He had two boys at home in the south of France, Louis and Leo. They lived with their mother Monique, from whom he had separated some time ago. The separation was neither peaceful nor happy. His life in the Foreign Legion and then in ECHO had ended any hope of their ever being happy together, as all Monique ever wanted was a normal family life following a promise from him to take up an ordinary job in the civilian world and retire from the Foreign Legion. When he had reneged on this, the trouble had started. Either way, he increasingly identified less and less as Reaper, having looked back on his life and wondered where all the years had gone. He began to doubt if he had spent them in the right way. When Monique had walked out, he had become Reaper permanently, because everyone he knew used that name and there was no one left in his life who called him Vincent.

Until now.

Scarlet Sloane called him Vincent although she sometimes used Reaper on a mission, but that was only at his insistence. It had become a running joke, but to him it was serious. It was Reaper who did these things, who was sometimes forced to shoot and stab people and set explosives, but never Vincent. Vincent's conscience was clear, but perhaps now he might let 'Reaper' go over time and go back to being the man he was before he joined the Legion.

"Turn left up here."

Shaken from his daydream, Reaper watched as Cairo turned the steering wheel and took the next left, just as Alex had told her. They had been cruising along 7th Ave, driving south towards their next destination in the meatpacking district, where Alex had told them they would be able to use the southern entrance to the Highline. Alex was navigating on her phone and now looked up and spoke once again to Scarlet.

"Another left here, Cairo," she said. "It's a parking garage on W 20th St and it's close to the park's southern entrance."

Scarlet pulled the car into the parking garage. "How much is this gonna cost?" she asked.

"It's twelve bucks an hour," Alex said. "I can pay on my phone when we leave."

THE MIDNIGHT SYNDICATE

Scarlet parked up the car and the three of them made their way to the southern entrance on Gansevoort Street. Entrance to the Highline was free, although the authorities did encourage people visiting the park to give a voluntary donation if they wanted to. Scarlet Sloane did not want to, as she marched straight into the park without even looking at any of the signs asking for donations. Behind her, Alex surreptitiously took $10 out of her wallet and posted it through one of the many onsite donation boxes near the entrance. Reaper caught her doing it and gave her a sly wink.

Scarlet was already marching up the stairs to the Highline, and when she reached the top she stepped into a completely different world to the rest of Manhattan. Suddenly she was surrounded by snow-covered plants giving the place a surreal, calm atmosphere which was further enhanced by several contemporary art installations dotted here and there along the Highline. She looked out to her left and took in an expansive and breathtaking view of the city and beyond it the Hudson River, but even in the cold, snowy weather there was already a bustling atmosphere in the park and Scarlet was soon irritated by having to weave through so many people to get further into the park.

She turned to Reaper and Alex. "Just how the fucking hell are we gonna find a telephone in all of this?"

"You're presuming it's another phone?" Reaper asked.

"Of course I am."

"I don't know where to start," Alex said. "Maybe we need to — "

Her words were ended by the sound of bullets firing into the air. She jumped and turned to see Reaper firing his Glock up into the snow clouds. The people on the Highline instantly screamed and sprinted for the exits and in less than twenty seconds they had the entire park to themselves.

"That's what we needed to do," Reaper said. "Now we've got the place to ourselves, but only for a few minutes before the cops turn up."

"Bloody hell, Vincent!" Scarlet said. "It could be hidden anywhere!"

"No, it won't be hidden anywhere," Reaper said with confidence. "It will be hidden somewhere almost in plain sight, just like the one in the fountain in the middle of Central Park. Remember they want us to find this thing.

So just get looking and we'll get it before the cops turn up, I promise."

Scarlet and Alex shrugged and knew they had no choice. Reaper had presented them with a fait accompli. He was French after all.

Scarlet took the left-hand side of the park, Alex took the right-hand side and Reaper ran ahead to the far end and worked backwards. Benches were situated here and there and along with the art installations and large rocks in some of the displays, these were one of the places all three of the ECHO members were careful to look in, but it was Reaper who found the phone taped to one of the handrails behind an art installation. He pulled out his knife and cut through the duct tape before throwing it to Scarlet."

In the background, they could already hear police sirens.

"Let's go!" Alex said.

Running towards the exit, Scarlet turned on the phone and all three of them stared down at the message.

"In King Kong's secret, you find your friends."

"What the hell does that mean?" Scarlet said as they rapidly descended the stairs and headed back to their parking garage.

"It's the 103rd floor at the Empire State Building," Alex said.

"I thought there were only 102 floors?" Reaper asked.

"That's the secret part. It's a secret floor," she added. "They built it as a point of embarkation for airships back in the day when they thought they were the future of travel. We need to go to the Empire State Building and we need to get to the secret floor on the 103rd level. That's where these assholes are keeping Kahlia and Ravi!"

CHAPTER TWENTY-TWO

The Witch Doctor had a magic box. This is where his black magic came from. From P=NP.

He was certain that he was the first person in the world to know this and it was this that had opened up his black magic box of tricks. Two weeks ago, P≠NP, or P was not equal to NP, but then all of a sudden, thanks to his hard work, P suddenly was equal to NP. The magic box was the key that solved this problem and gave the Witch Doctor his new formidable black magic power. More powerful than any plague, more devastating than any nuclear weapon.

And how he enjoyed using that power.

Now things that had once been very hard or almost impossible were the easiest thing in the world to understand. But the Witch Doctor had much to learn about his new box of tricks and had always to keep one eye on the Director, for it was he who called the tune. He broadly agreed with the Director's vision for the world, but there were disagreements between the two of them. Nothing serious, the Witch Doctor mused, but perhaps they might become more serious in time. He wondered how these differences might be settled, and wondered if he could break away from the Director. It would be possible, but only when he knew more about how the magic box worked, what was inside it and what its full potential was. For now, the Director had him at a distinct disadvantage on the matter.

There was, after all, no honour among thieves.

The Witch Doctor realised that he was thirsty. He often was so engrossed in his work that he forgot to eat or even drink, sometimes for hours and hours. He struggled out of his chair and waddled across his room to a small chrome refrigerator which he opened and after a few seconds fussing around on the shelves, pulled out an ice-cold bottle of Corona lager. He also pulled out a greasy cardboard box which contained the second half of a pizza that he had started the night before. He positioned the bottle of Corona down against the kitchen sideboard, so the edge of the cap was resting just against it and then smacked down on the lid with his palm to knock the lid off. As the lid rolled onto the floor, it spun around and disappeared under the refrigerator, he walked back to his chair with the pizza box and the cold lager. He slumped down in the chair, slapped the cardboard box on the side next to his magic box of spells, opened it up and tore himself off a greasy slice of the pepperoni pizza. The cold pepperoni pizza. Then he took a bite, taking nearly half the slice off in one go, began to chew it and then washed it down with an enormous glug of the cold beer. He belched loudly, finished the pizza slice and set his beer down on the desk. The Witch Doctor turned to face his magic box of spells.

He had been sitting at his desk in Shangri La for what seemed like forever now, but it would all be worth it in the end. And there was something strangely alluring about the magic box of tricks. Something that the Witch Doctor was so fascinated by, that he sometimes spent weeks on end without seeing daylight, simply hunched over his desk working that strange black magic. He opened what he sometimes called his 'grimoire' and looked through his notes until he found the hex he was looking for. For a moment he was too scared to cast it, but he knew he had the blessing of the Director. His explicit orders. Disobeying him was not an option.

Unless he allied with the magic box. Then the world was his.

All thanks to P=NP.

CHAPTER TWENTY-THREE

As they drove, Hawke gazed through the car window and watched the New York streets flash past, block after block. Ryan was at the wheel now, talking mostly to himself about the cosmic censorship hypothesis as he steered the vehicle through the traffic almost subconsciously. Lea was in the back, her eyes glued to her phone's screen as she gave her ex-husband directions.

Not for the first time this mission, Hawke found his mind wandering. In the quieter moments they shared, Lea had started talking to him about starting a family. It wasn't the first time she had mentioned it to him, but she had begun to talk about it more consistently lately and Hawke understood why – neither of them were getting any younger. He also understood it would mean the end of ECHO because there was no way he would ever contemplate bringing up a child in such an environment. Lea felt the same and they had tentatively discussed leaving Elysium together to bring up their children either in Ireland or England. Conversations on the subject hadn't pinned down exactly which one of these countries they would settle in.

These conversations were between the two of them, with no one else on the ECHO team, from Sir Richard Eden at the top down to newcomers Ravi and Kahlia having the slightest idea that there was a chance, however small, that he and Lea might be considering leaving the team. This was the reason they never discussed it on a mission, but only in those quiet, private moments back on Elysium when they were in their separate part of the compound. Neither was so conceited or vain that they thought exiting the team would mean the end of ECHO, but they both had trouble visualising Richard directing missions against increasingly hostile enemies without either of their inputs. Perhaps leaving would be for the best, Hawke thought, for this very reason. It would allow Richard to recruit two new senior operatives to lead his team in the field – younger, stronger people with new blood might be exactly what the team needed at this point in its existence.

"What do you think we might find when we get there?"

Hawke turned to Lea. "A heavily defended property full of extremely high-tech equipment is my best bet."

"Mine too," Ryan added. "Which is why I wish Cairo, Reaper and Alex were with us."

"It's just as important that they rescue Ravi and Kahlia," Hawke said.

"But that's exactly why these bastards wanted us to split the team, divide our power. Divide and conquer!" Ryan said.

"Whether they wanted us to do it or not is irrelevant," Lea said. "It's irrelevant because Joe's right – there's a timer counting down on the lives of Ravi and Kahlia and we're not going to sacrifice them just to give us a slightly better chance or slightly better odds when we reach the warehouse. That's not who we are."

"Yeah, and those bastards exploited that," Ryan said.

"Them's the breaks, Ryan," Lea said, returning her eyes to her telephone. "It's the next left by the way."

Ryan dabbed the brakes and pulled into the left turn lane, but was a little too late to make it through the lights. Now they waited impatiently at the red signal waiting for it to turn green. Ryan drummed his fingers on the top of the steering wheel. Hawke closed his eyes and began to prepare for the attack on the warehouse. The only sound in the car was the occasional tap of Lea's fingernail as she worked on her telephone.

"You ever get sick of going after these arseholes?" Ryan asked out of nowhere.

Hawke felt Lea's eyes burning a hole through his neck. Without turning to her he said, "It's what we do Ryan."

"And there's no one else who can do it as well as us," Lea said. "There's lots of secondary teams out there working for various governments or private contractors, off the books… you know how it works, but they don't get the results we do. We're the tip of the spear! So if we don't do it who else is going to?"

Good answer Hawke thought. But was it the truth? If what Lea had said to him about wanting to leave the team to start a family was true, then she was merely telling Ryan what he wanted to hear. But what if there was even just a small part of what she had said that was true?

The lights changed. Ryan switched his foot from the brake pedal to the throttle and the old stolen Chevy pulled gently away across the junction before he turned smoothly to the left and began driving west through Manhattan towards the Hudson River.

"We're almost there," Lea said a few moments later, as they pulled into a decidedly down-market part of the city. As the luxurious townhouses and skyscrapers of Manhattan slowly turned into old red brick industrial properties, the sky seemed to darken and a fresh flurry of snow tumbled out of the heavens and blasted over their car, causing Ryan to switch the windscreen wipers on once again.

While Hawke was always up for a fight, he had to admit, at least inwardly to himself, that he was feeling the rough and tumble of these missions more and more with each one. He had a pain in his lower back and his arms were aching just from the relatively short fight earlier. As Ryan turned into the industrial estate, he gazed out through the falling snow towards a black van parked up on their left about one hundred yards ahead of them.

"That's Cambridge's GMC van," Hawke said. "We've got the bastards."

CHAPTER TWENTY-FOUR

Hawke pulled up out of sight behind the warehouse and killed the engine. The three of them climbed out of the car and closed the doors. They took in the building. Snowflakes drifted down past the backdrop of the Manhattan skyline but never settled on its corrugated steel roof as it had on all the other surrounding buildings.

"Bit of a giveaway that it's heated and not abandoned," Hawke said, pointing. "But you can't get everything right."

Lea and Ryan nodded in understanding.

The rest of the warehouse was typical for the location, with a large rectangular footprint set back from the road and partially obscured behind a solid metal fence. The supporting exterior walls were made of the kind of red bricks ubiquitous to so much of the Big Apple, but these were badly weathered, covered in cracks and graffiti and the sections at the base covered in concrete showed signs of significant spalling to the point of exposing rust-flecked steel reinforcement rods, like skeletons protruding from a corpse. Topping it all off was an exposed electrical conduit on the far wall.

"Cosy," Ryan said.

"It all looks a little too abandoned if you ask me," said Lea, shivering with the cold.

"Agreed," Hawke said. "A lot of effort to go to only to let yourself down with shitty roof insulation. This is the place, all right."

"I think calling it Shangri La was a tad optimistic," Ryan said with a laugh.

Hawke smiled but said nothing. He was taking in the intricate crisscross of concrete joists and steel trusses that were now visible on the roof thanks to a missing section of the steel corrugated sheets that covered the rest.

Hawke walked around to the back of the Chevy and opened up the tailgate door. Leaning inside, he felt temporary relief from the icy wind and zipped open the small weapons bags on the carpeted floor panel of the boot. Lea and Ryan wandered over to him and he handed each of them a Glock, then he gave each of them two stun grenades before taking the same for himself, plus an additional MP5 which he slung over his shoulder before closing the boot and turning to face the others.

"There's something about this place that bothers me," he said bluntly. "I don't know what it is, but it's just a feeling I have when I look at it. For one thing, it's too quiet and for another, like we've already said, it's far too obvious that it's been made to look abandoned. They may as well have sent out gold-embossed invitations to us."

"I agree," Lea said. "And it wasn't exactly difficult tracing Cambridge and his van to this place either. That's what bothers me."

Ryan shuffled to keep warm and shoved his gloved hands into his pockets, his right hand still gripping the Glock Hawke had just given him. "We haven't got any other play at the moment. This is the place where the trail has led us and we don't have any other leads. We just have to go in there."

"We're going in there all right," Hawke said, spoiling for a fight. "And hard and fast. All I'm saying is that I've got a bad feeling when I look at this place. We've driven around the place so we know there's only one way in and that's through this main entrance, which is adding to my sense of uneasiness. We can see they've got cameras up there so they're gonna know we're here, but judging from their performance back in Manhattan with the LED billboard, it's perfectly feasible to imagine they've got control of all of the CCTV cameras around here and not just those restricted to their ownership. They might have tracked us from when we started today."

"You're filling me with hope and joy, Josiah."

"You're welcome." Hawke checked his weapon was ready to fire and stepped off the road onto the pavement. The snow turned into a blizzard. "All right, everyone let's do it – and keep your wits about you. There's something about this just isn't right."

CHAPTER TWENTY-FIVE

Sitting in his private quarters in Shangri La, the man known as the Director was contemplating the exigencies of his command over the Midnight Syndicate when the call came in from his second-in-command. Leaning forward in his seat, the leather creased and squeaked as he reached for the intercom on his desk.

"Speak."

"The ECHO team are preparing to attack, sir. I can see them here on screen G15."

"You're certain?"

"Yes, sir. They're on the street outside the warehouse."

"I'm on my way."

The walk was not long. The Director had simply to leave his quarters and walk along a windowless corridor. From here, he took a lift up to ground level. When he stepped out, he took another corridor, lined on one side by windows made almost opaque by the blizzard outside. Then he arrived, three minutes later, in the control room.

"Here, sir," the man said, tapping one of the screens. "You can see for yourself."

The Director stepped over to the man and looked at the screen for himself. There, he saw, sure enough, the figures of Hawke, Lea and Ryan armed to the teeth and preparing an ingress on the west side of the building. They wore hoods, but their faces were still visible, and they had pistols in their hands. Hawke had what looked like a compact machine pistol – maybe an MP5 – on a strap over his shoulder. They moved with a purpose that both impressed and unnerved the Director. Despite the heavy snow, the image was still clear enough to enable him to make out their faces and get a positive ID on them. Watching them closely as they drew closer to the compound, the Director ordered the man sitting in front of the CCTV monitors to rotate one of the cameras and zoom in on Hawke's face.

"That's them all right," he said. "They arrived quicker than I thought."

"What are your orders, sir?"

The Director considered the question without hesitation. "I don't want any of them getting anywhere near us," he said coldly. "We're too close to initiating the final solution to be taken down now by this grotty little band of riff-raff. And we definitely don't want them getting to Haggblom."

This raised an ironic, grim laugh in the tense room.

"This means take them out," the Director said, confirming his intentions with icy clarity.

"Should we send the Cayman Crew out after them?"

"No, that won't be possible – they're dealing with another problem. Use the remote-controlled machine guns – the ones mounted on tripods concealed below the roofline."

"Sir, once we make them operational they'll rise and become visible above the roofline. This will give away their position and let the enemy know we're aware of their presence. You sure you want me to make these weapons operational?"

The Director felt anger rising inside him. "I wouldn't have told you to do it if I wasn't sure. They're already too close and clearly, they know that they found the right place. So do as I say and activate the tripod-mounted remote-controlled machine guns at once."

The man obeyed, striking a key on his keyboard and a second later three more CCTV monitors flickered to life in front of him as the machine guns were raised above the level of the roof line on struts. Now the man activated the weapons system fully and turned the three submachine guns, dotted along the top of the warehouse roof, until Hawke, Lea and Ryan became visible in the sights, now viewable on the monitors in front of them.

The Director stared blankly at the face of Joe Hawke, partly obscured by his hood as he raised his pistol into the aim and jogged right across the middle of the warehouse's loading dock.

"I am beginning to hate that man," he said. "He is as bold as brass. Now kill him."

"Sir." The man activated the three machine guns and the Director watched as the three M240s spat a lethal fusillade of 7.62mm rounds all over the loading dock, firing up bursts of snow as they tracked closer to Hawke, Lea and Ryan now sprinting faster to evade being struck.

The Director watched as the man expertly re-sited the automatic weapons, this time closing in on the man at the back – Ryan Bale. He let rip another short burst of rounds and the Director watched in pleasure as the blurry black and white figure tracking across the snowy loading bay now clutched his leg and fell onto the concrete.

"Is that Bale?" Director said.

"Yes, sir," the man said. "I can confirm Bale has taken a bullet and he's on the ground."

The Director was satisfied with their defences. "Good work. Now kill him and then take out Hawke and Donovan. Then I want the Midnight Syndicate in the conference room to discuss the next phase of our operations."

"Sir."

Then the Director turned and walked calmly out of the room.

CHAPTER TWENTY-SIX

When Scarlet reached the Empire State Building's Observation Deck, she saw it was unhelpfully full of people enjoying the spectacle of a blizzard over New York City. From what Alex had told her, they would have to cross the deck and then somehow get through a private and almost certainly locked door which would then lead up to the 102nd Floor, a small area with a window running 360 degrees around it. From here, they would then have to ascend another set of stairs, this time private and with no public access and so almost certainly locked, to reach the secret 103rd Floor, where the final riddle had promised they would find Ravi and Kahlia.

She was barely halfway across the Observation Deck when she saw someone who did not fit in. He was a tall man with blond hair cut short, combed back and styled with grease. He was very tall and well-built with ice-cold blue eyes. He was wearing a black roll-neck under a black jacket, under which he was almost certainly concealing a shoulder rig. She recognised the boots as those worn by the men she had encountered earlier and saw he had a small earpiece in his left ear. Compounding her suspicions were two other women, dressed similarly to him and also wearing earpieces in their ears. She thought she saw one of the women reaching inside her jacket and not to be outdone in the quick draw department, reached for her Glock.

An arms race ensued and shots were soon fired.

Everyone in the crowd screamed and ran for their lives.

Scarlet didn't hold back and fired on the mercenaries with a vengeance. With one magazine, she killed two of the men and injured a third, sending the remaining Cayman Crew mercs running for cover. Behind her, men, women and children were now streaming through the exits, but Scarlet and her small team ran the other way, closing in on the mercenaries who now turned and took cover inside the Observation Deck.

Scarlet now changed mags, and launched herself through the air, emptying another dozen or so rounds at one of the surviving mercenaries as she crashed back to the floor. After executing a perfect sideways roll, she sprang to her feet and hit a female merc in the face with the butt of her pistol before she had a chance to reload her gun. She staggered back, tottering on her heels with a smashed nose and blood streaming down her mouth.

To her right, Reaper was now grappling with a male mercenary. Scarlet saw he was being forced to use every ounce of strength in his body to bring the much bigger man under control, as he brought his arms up and pummelled him in the head and chest with a series of unrelenting blows which seemed to have barely any effect at all on the mercenary.

"Kill him Dresden!" the female merc cried out.

"With pleasure, Paris..." the man said, taking another swing at Reaper.

Alex was having an even tougher time on Scarlet's left, where another female mercenary was easily getting the better of her. This merc was short but built like a tank and clearly stronger and more powerfully built, not to mention a significantly superior martial artist. This meant she had little trouble slapping Alex around, knocking her off of her feet and sending her crashing onto the floor whenever she pleased. Scarlet was fully engaged in fighting her opponent, the one the man named Dresden had called Paris and could do nothing except call over to Alex when she saw her strength waning, trying to motivate her by screaming her name and telling her she could win. Scarlet had already observed Alex's opponent's weak point, which was her overconfidence which led her to defend herself poorly when attacking Alex.

"You can do it, Alex! Exploit her arrogance!"

Dresden laughed. "You hear that, Moscow – you're arrogant!"

Scarlet's momentary distraction in trying to help her teammate had cost her. Paris lashed out and Scarlet felt a hefty punch in her sternum which knocked her off her feet and sent her crashing down onto the ground, landing with a thud on her backside. She had no time to feel sorry for herself because Paris was already stomping over to her and pulling a combat knife from a utility belt around her waist. Scarlet heard Reaper grunting behind her, still engaged in the fight with Dresden and she turned to see both men rolling on the floor, piling fists into each other's faces. She winced when she saw Dresden land a punch squarely on Reaper's nose, wondering if it might have been hard enough to set it straight again. She had no time to check on Scarlet as Paris was now upon her again, slashing a knife in the air inches from her face.

Paris had underestimated Scarlet's strength, and now the Englishwoman slid forward and hooked Paris's legs out from under her, sending her tumbling backwards onto the ground. At the same time, Scarlet sprang to her feet and now found herself once again with the upper hand over her opponent. She strode forward and savagely kicked the combat knife out of Paris's hand, then as her opponent got up to her hands and knees, halfway on her way up to her feet, Scarlet aimed at the woman's rib cage and kicked her as hard as she could, as if pretending she was kicking a ball across a football field, aiming the kick right through her.

The heavy impact of Scarlet's boot against the woman's rib had the desired effect, and now she heard a dry cracking sound and Paris cried out in pain. She tumbled over onto her back, doubled over and cradled her rib cage, giving Scarlet the time she needed to reload her weapon and snatch up the combat knife that she had kicked away from her moments before. She wasted no time, leaning forward and landing a hefty punch on Paris's temple, knocking her clean out. Then she turned to survey the carnage unfolding across the remainder of the Observation Deck.

Reaper seemed to have got the better of Dresden, who was now lying on the floor face up with Reaper hunched over him landing blow after blow, one on the left side then one on the right side of his head. After a few seconds of this, he knocked Dresden out and now he got up, stretched up to his full height, dusted his hands off and asked if Scarlet was OK.

Scarlet said she was, then the two of them ran over to Alex who was still being given a hard time by the female mercenary called Moscow. As they walked over to her, Scarlet watched as Alex somehow managed to gain the advantage for the first time since her opponent had so deftly disarmed her of her Glock and booted it out of reach. Now, Alex swiped a blade at Moscow's bloodied face, but the Russian had anticipated the move and flicked her head back out of reach of the lethal weapon. Scarlet was on the verge of grabbing the Russian from behind and pulling her away from her friend when Alex somehow managed to turn the tables using a second thrust of the knife but this time as a faint. Alex then brought her left boot up between Moscow's legs as hard as she could and brought her knife-free hand up into her throat at the same time, landing a tiger punch directly on the mercenary's windpipe.

Moscow fell backwards, her face contorted with an anguished expression as her brain processed the pain between her legs and the terrible crushing blow in her throat. When she hit the polished floor of the Observation Deck, her attempt to arrest her fall by throwing out her arms was not enough to stop the back of her skull from cracking on the hard tiles. At that instant, her eyes rolled back into her head and she died there and then on the floor, inches from Alex's boots.

"I didn't mean to kill her," Alex said, her face almost as anguished as Moscow's face was a few seconds before. "But I had to do it, right?"

Scarlet saw her friend was deeply troubled by how she had dispatched the Russian mercenary. Behind Alex, through the glass window of the Observation Deck, the swelling snowstorm over New York had worsened since their arrival at the Empire State Building, and now much of the city's famous skyline was obscured from view by the blizzard. Somehow this seemed to reflect the confused pain in Alex's eyes as she continued to stare at her and

Reaper for some kind of reassurance that she had done the right thing.

After glancing at the unconscious bodies of Paris and Dresden, Scarlet said, "She would have rammed that knife through your ribcage in a heartbeat, Alex. Don't you ever think you did the wrong thing!"

Reaper was nodding and walked over to Alex, putting his large bare-like hand on her shoulder to give her some physical comfort alongside the supportive words uttered seconds ago by Scarlet.

"Tu as fait la bonne chose, mon ami," he said. "You always do the right thing."

"Thanks," was all Alex said, still staring at Moscow.

The brevity of the reply suited Scarlet just fine – they still had to climb one more floor up to the secret 103rd Floor and see if the Cayman Crew had been truthful when telling them their friends were being held there with the explosives in their backpacks.

"C'mon, let's get up there and make sure Ravi and Kahlia are okay," she said. "Then we can regroup with Hawke and send the rest of these bastards to the same place old Moscow just went."

Reaper took his hand off Alex's shoulder and spoke for the first time since the fatal punch. "My thoughts exactly," he said. "To Hell."

CHAPTER TWENTY-SEVEN

Scarlet led the charge through the locked gate, which she unlocked with her gun, and up the narrow steep metal stairs to the 103rd Floor of the Empire State Building. Up here there was no public access, except for specially and previously arranged visits usually from rich celebrities. There was a good reason for that and Scarlet saw why when she took her Glock and blew the lock off the final door and stepped outside.

She was practically at the very top of the skyscraper, with nothing above her except for the metal point. The whole of New York City stretched out far below in every direction and she looked down to see that she was standing in a tiny circular walkway only two feet wide and with nothing but a waist-high barrier between her and the ground hundreds of feet below. The wind was savage, cutting across her and forcing her to cling onto the handrail for all her life was worth as the snow blasted her from every direction. Worse than any of that, there was no sight of Kahlia or Ravi. Had DC and the Cayman Crew betrayed them? Was all of this nothing more than a wild goose chase to mess them around and split the team up, weakening their forces and slowing their ability to track down the Crew itself?

Realising that the narrow walkway formed a perfect circle around the very top of the building, she knew there was one chance left to find her teammates, and now clinging onto the handrail with a numb hand and holding her Glock firmly in the other, she bowed her head against the whipping snow and made her way around the circular walkway. When she reached the far side of the entrance she had just used, she felt an enormous wave of relief when she saw Ravi and Kahlia. They had been sat down by their kidnappers on the walkway and tied back to back. They still had gags in their mouths and they were still blindfolded, they were encrusted in snow and turning blue from the cold. They had split lips and some bruising on their faces. The two backpacks that had been on their backs had now been taped with duct tape to their fronts, enabling the Cayman Crew's mercs to tie them together in this way.

Seeing there was no enemy up here, and knowing Paris and Dresden would be out for a good deal longer, Scarlet now holstered her Glock and knelt in front of Kahlia who was facing her and tore off the blindfold. Kahlia screamed through her gag and blinked wildly, flashing her head from side to side in terror until she realised she was staring into the eyes of Cairo Sloane. Scarlet now tore the gag from her mouth and pressed her hands against her temples, holding her head still and trying to warm up her ears.

"You're okay Kahlia, darling," Scarlet said. "I'm here with Reap and Alex. You're going to be okay."

As she spoke, Scarlet saw Reaper's figure appear in front of her. He had gone the other way around the circular walkway and was now standing in front of Ravi, still gripping his Glock, raised into the aim and ready to fire. When he saw Scarlet and the hostages, he holstered his weapon and repeated the process she had done, but with Ravi.

"Where's Alex?" Kahlia asked.

"She's guarding the door that leads up here," Reaper said. "Just in case those bastards can mount a second wave attack."

"You should have killed them," Ravi said.

"They're unconscious," Reaper said. "We don't shoot unconscious people."

"Where is DC?" Kahlia asked.

"No idea," Reaper said. "Probably down in a van coordinating the others."

Scarlet was vaguely taking in the conversation but her attention was focused on the worrying digital numbers on the timer on top of the explosives inside the backpack on Kahlia's lap. What she saw made the blood in her veins run as cold as the snow and ice tearing across the top of the skyscraper, and scouring their faces. She saw from the look on Reaper's face that he had also made the same discovery.

Three minutes and twelve seconds until the detonation.

"They changed the countdown," Kahlia said. "They reset it to go off earlier."

"Bastards!" Reaper said.

"What the hell are we going to do?" Kahlia asked.

Scarlet was shaking her head. "We can't throw them over the side of the building. We wouldn't be able to hurl them out far enough not to cause massive damage to the building and anyone inside that floor. And there's no way we can leave them up here to blow the top off the building, and there's nowhere we can get away fast enough. We'll be killed in the explosion as we try and run."

"There's still a chance," Kahlia said desperately. "They can be deactivated if we answer a riddle. Dresden told me when he was tying me up."

"Riddle?" Scarlet asked, already annoyed by the prospect. "Another fucking riddle?"

"I don't know," Kahlia said. "I haven't seen it yet! Like I said, it's just what one of those bastards told us when they forced us up here and taped us together like this."

"Do you have any idea what this riddle is?" Reaper asked Ravi.

The Brazilian shook his head. "No, it's just like Kahlia said. They forced us up here at gunpoint, taped us together, put the explosives on our laps and told us that we needed to answer a riddle to shut these things down. And there's a lot of explosives, Reap."

"I'll say there's a lot of fucking explosives," Scarlet said. "There's enough here to take out the top quarter of the Empire State Building. They'll be picking pieces of it up in Queens."

Scarlet searched the backpack and then found what she was looking for – it wasn't hard because they wanted her to find it. She now stared at the simple piece of paper with handwriting haphazardly scrawled on it. The riddle.

"What does it say?" Kahlia asked.

Scarlet furrowed her brow. "Only meditation can coordinate you with Descartes to stop the explosion and survive."

"What the hell?" Reaper said.

Scarlet sighed heavily and shook her head, reading it out one more time.

"Anyone know what this could mean?" Scarlet said.

Reaper shrugged his shoulders. "Sorry, but no. I'd need longer than three minutes to think about it anyway."

"Two minutes and fifty-one seconds actually," Scarlet said correcting him.

"Read it again," Kahlia said.

Scarlet read the riddle again, but this time Kahlia and Ravi both said they had no idea either.

"Alex, get your arse around here right now!" Scarlet yelled.

Alex appeared, and then Scarlet read out the riddle to her.

Scarlet looked up at Alex; she had spent a long time working for various government agencies, specifically in the areas of cryptography and she had a polymath mind like her boyfriend Ryan. Everyone knew she was their only real hope in a situation like this.

"You must coordinate yourselves to stop the explosion and survive," Alex said to herself. Then she repeated it one more time – you must coordinate yourselves to stop the explosion and survive."

"Two and a half minutes, Alex!" Scarlet said.

"It's a reference to Cartesian coordinates," Alex said. "Descartes's most famous philosophical work was called his 'meditations'. They're telling us to use Cartesian coordinates – that's three-dimensional coordinates using an XYZ axis, I mean if we want to survive and get out of here."

"Of course, we want to fucking survive!" Scarlet said.

"You mean like geographical coordinates?" Reaper asked, reaching for his phone to get GPS coordinates for their location.

"Yes, I think so," Alex said.

"No, that can't be it," said Scarlet. "It looks like we need seven digits to deactivate this. No set of geographical coordinates could be that small, and even if we truncated them somehow we wouldn't know which ones to use. You need to think again, Alex. And fast! There's less than two minutes left before we go sky high."

Alex cursed and her face folded into a confused mess. "I was certain I had it right. About the Cartesian coordinates, I mean."

Scarlet's blood ran cold as the timer raced its way down to double digits. "Fifty-five seconds, Alex. We're not getting out of here now – not on foot, anyway."

"We wouldn't even get down to the Observation Deck," Reaper said. As he spoke, he finished the job of cutting through the duct tape holding Ravi and Kahlia to one another. Then he cut the packs of explosives from their laps and set them to the side."

Alex's face suddenly was illuminated with hope, reminding Scarlet of sunlight bursting through a break in the clouds. "I have it! I was right – they are looking for Cartesian coordinates of a kind, just not geographical ones. You said there are seven spaces for digits, is that right?"

Scarlet nodded. "Yes, and we need to be pretty bloody sharpish about typing them in because we're under thirty seconds."

"Then type in 2034103," Alex said. "That's for 20 W, 34th Street, and Floor 103! Cartesian XYZ axis coordinates of our current location."

"I hope you're right." Scarlet followed her instructions, typing the numbers into each of the explosives timers. But the digits continued to work. "No dice, Alex. It hasn't worked."

Scarlet had a final, desperate thought about hurling the packs over the side, but knew she could never do any such thing. Yes, it would save their lives but explosives of such a quantity detonating halfway down the Empire State Building, right outside someone's residential apartment on one of the floors below, was not something that she could live with.

"Then type in 103 3420!" Alex said, her voice rising almost to a shout.

Scarlet typed it in and once again the action failed to stop the whirring numbers.

"Ten seconds, Alex," Scarlet said. "It was a privilege working with you all."

Time seemed to stop. Scarlet, Alex, Ravi, Kahlia and Reaper stared at each other in the snowy silence. Scarlet fixed her eyes on Reaper, a man with whom she had finally found love after decades of searching. In less than ten seconds they would all be blown into thousands of pieces, along with a good chunk of the top of the Empire State Building.

"Damn it, Cairo!" Alex said. "Then type in 34 20 103!"

Scarlet tapped in the numbers as fast as she could, just as Alex had told her. With the horrifying spectacle of the numbers 00:00:00:7 on the readout in front of her, encrusted with snow, the numbers suddenly stopped.

"Did it work?" Alex asked.

Scarlet said nothing in response. She wiped snow from her eyes, her hands trembling with cold and fear.

Ravi leaned forward and saw the number seven at the end of the display. "Only seven seconds to go? That was a close shave."

"Wrong," Scarlet said coldly as she slowly got to her feet. "Look again, Ravi – that's seven-tenths of a second remaining."

No one said anything else all the way down to the ground.

CHAPTER TWENTY-EIGHT

Storming across the warehouse loading dock, Hawke saw the bullets strike Ryan out of the corner of his eye and turned in time to see his old friend hit the deck, exposed and vulnerable to a lethal shot. He screamed at Lea to carry on until she hit what they thought was a blind spot on the warehouse wall and standby, and then he slung his weapon over his shoulder and sprinted across to Ryan. Grabbing him by his ankles, and under heavy fire from the machine guns up on the roof, he dragged him through the snow until they were behind a rusted dumpster. He began checking Ryan's wounds.

"That wasn't very fucking clever, was it, Rupert?"

Ryan smiled, then cried out in pain. "Are you trying to feel me up? Because if you are, I've had better."

"I find that hard to believe," Hawke said, continuing to check Ryan's arms, legs and body for any life-threatening wounds besides the obvious shot in the lower leg. The gallows humour was helping them both.

"Do I need a doctor or a vicar?"

"Looks like you've taken a bullet in the left calf, mate. You need a doctor, but all you've got for now is an old bootneck with some ancient battlefield medic training. How does that grab you?"

"It grabs me all right, a bit like your hands on my nuts a few seconds ago."

Hawke laughed. Having easily found the entry wound, he was now looking once again for an exit wound just in case he missed it. He had not. "I was checking your femoral artery, you pillock. Don't go anywhere."

"Joe!"

Hawke darted to his right and checked around the side of the dumpster. Lea was in position in the blind spot, up against the warehouse wall, breathing hard, her gun still gripped in her hand as the snow tumbled down in thick flurries. Hawke gave her a thumbs up and raised three fingers on his right hand, indicating how long he would be. She nodded once. Hawke returned to Ryan.

"How's my little soldier?" he asked.

"In agony. How's Lea?" Ryan asked.

"She's hanging on." Hawke was now controlling the bleeding from Ryan's leg by wrapping some webbing from his combat jacket around it and trying to stem the flow of blood with the added pressure. "She probably hasn't been through anything this traumatic since her marriage to you."

Ryan was wincing in pain. "Is this your idea of what good bedside manner is supposed to be like?"

Both men heard more gunfire from inside the warehouse then the sound of Lea returning fire. Then, more silence.

Hawke dragged an old winter tyre off a pile behind them and positioned it so he could rest Ryan's foot on it, elevating the wound in the calf. Then he checked his vital signs once more. All was stable. "Now then, mate – as your doctor, I'm advising you to stay put for the remainder of today's fun and japes. You've got a lovely, cosy little place here by the dumpster and some nice old tyres for company, so you should be okay till I get back."

"Unless you get yourself killed."

Hawke smiled. "C'mon, Rupert... don't say that! Where's your spirit of adventure?"

"On the other side of the yard with half of my leg."

"Good lad!"

Before Ryan could reply, Hawke was gone, breaking cover from the dumpster and sprinting through the blizzard towards Lea.

Slamming up against the wall beside her, Hawke asked her if she was okay. She gave him a quick nod and he knew her well enough that he needed to ask no more. Then she asked him about Ryan.

"You know Ryan," Hawke said. "The little shit will do anything to get out of a day's work."

Lea smiled but could not bring herself to laugh. The two of them quickly decided on the best way to storm the warehouse, and then make their move, breaking cover from the blind spot beneath a camera on the southern wall and opening fire on the padlock hasp, blowing it to pieces. Then they fired on a deadbolt lock beneath it, rapidly shredding the lock and allowing them to kick open the warehouse door. Hawke had already torn a grenade from his combat vest and now pulled the pin and threw it inside, before slamming himself back up against the outside wall. Other side of the door Lea did the same, her gun clasped in front of her ready for battle.

Hawke said, "We go in three, two, one — "

The Director was pleased with events so far, if a little unhappy at being called back into the control room. The kidnapping in New York had gone well and was already bearing dividends. DC had reported the death of a member of the Cayman Crew, but this was mere collateral damage. They had the Crucible and all of the research, all of which was being transported inside the briefcase. All they needed now was a few finishing touches and they would be ready to move on with the main operation.

"They're right outside the door on the southern wall now, sir."

The Director leaned into the CCTV cameras and allowed his eyes to settle once more on the figures of Joe Hawke and Lea Donovan. As had just been explained to him, the two of them were standing beside the double doors on the southern wall of the warehouse.

"And the other one? Is he still wounded?"

"Yes, sir. He's out of sight on the far side far side of the yard. He's behind the row of dumpsters over there."

"And we can't reach him with any of our weapons?"

"No, not while he's behind the dumpsters. But the second he comes out, he's dead meat."

"What are the other two doing now?"

"Preparing to attack," the man said, using the small joystick on his desk to zoom in on Hawke and Lea until their faces filled the CCTV screen. "It looks like they're discussing something, sir. Probably the best way to attack."

"Zoom back out again," the Director said. "Hawke's moving his shoulder. I want to see what he's up to."

The Director watched as the man operating the CCTV camera pulled back on the joystick and zoomed back the camera lens until they were able to see Hawke and Lea from their waists up. It was clear now that Hawke was pulling something from the combat vest he was wearing. It looked like a grenade.

"Okay, the attack is imminent," the Director said. "That is a grenade. Prepare our defences as best as you can. We'll only get one chance to kill them both and when they're both dead I want the one hiding behind the dumpsters also taken out. Then finally I might be able to get on with more important work."

"Sir."

"I'll be with the Midnight Syndicate, but if they get inside I am to be called at once.'

And with that, the Director strolled calmly away from the control room and disappeared.

CHAPTER TWENTY-NINE

Hawke and Lea now exchanged a knowing glance and then closed their eyes just as the explosion detonated inside the warehouse, blasting a powerful cloud of smoke and other pieces of detritus through the door at incredible speed. Before the smoke had time to dissipate, the two battle-hardened warriors spun around from their positions and raked the inside of the warehouse with rounds. After a few seconds, Hawke ran forward into the warehouse and sprayed more rounds in an arcing motion from left to right, using the cloud of grenade smoke as cover. Behind him, he heard Lea fitting a new magazine into her gun and then she ran into the warehouse and joined him with another intense burst of fire.

With sharp senses and nerves of steel, they edged forward through the smoke and soon realised the main warehouse was devoid of life, not because they had killed anyone inside it, but because it had been empty right from the start. Turning to look at each other with looks of confusion on their faces, they walked towards an industrial metal staircase on the far wall that seemed to lead up to what looked like a small suite of offices.

Hawke was halfway up the stairs when the sound of gunfire once again exploded all around them, shattering the eerie calm inside the warehouse and forcing both of them to sprint up the staircase as fast as possible to what they hoped was the safety of the offices. It was their only play because the rest of the warehouse was empty and offered no cover. As they sprinted up the stairs, their boots pounding on the steel steps and making the entire structure rock and sway, Hawke saw there was another machine gun fitted to the ceiling of the warehouse at the far end, obscured behind a sheet of steel with only a slit to fire through. Now it was firing on them with a vengeance. There was no way to strike its operator, there was only time to heave himself up onto the top landing and then kick his way into one of the offices. Lea joined him seconds later, just in time to avoid another wild barrage of gunfire as it raked the office windows and shattered them into a million shards of glass, which now rained down all over the top of them as they crawled for the safety of a desk in the corner.

"Just what the hell was that?" Lea asked.

"Some kind of a machine gun nest up at the far corner of the main warehouse," Hawke said.

"You see who was firing it?"

Hawke shook his head. "No, just didn't have time."

Before Lea could ask him the obvious question, Hawke put his head above the parapet by raising himself on his knees and opening fire on the machine gun nest in the far corner of the warehouse. The bullets raked the far wall, drilling into the steel and eventually met their mark, hitting the steel shield and then penetrating the gap and blasting the machine gun to pieces, finally rendering it inoperable. Hawke slumped back down onto the ground beside Lea and switched his magazines, slapping a new one into the receiver frame of his weapon.

He stared up at the ceiling, a gently sloping affair with a thick plastic skylight now covered in snow, which gave the office only the dimmest and creepiest lighting. Staring at Lea's face in the gloom he started speaking.

"I think this is a trap. I think we were lured here on purpose. To me, this entire place is rigged with remote-controlled weapons. Think about it! First, we had the three machine guns up on the roof pouring some pretty heavy fire on us but at no point did we see any of the operators. Then we burst in here and the place is completely deserted, and then when we started climbing up the stairs to the office, they opened fire on us again with a machine gun nest in the far corner of the warehouse, also unmanned. This whole place is a trap."

"Congratulations, Mr Hawke."

Hawke and Lea stared up at the voice booming as if it was God's, filling the warehouse. It didn't take either of them long to find the speaker concealed in the ceiling of the office, but the voice sounded distorted like it was being run through some kind of voice changer.

"Is that DC's voice?" Lea whispered.

Hawke shrugged, then raised his voice. "If I can hear you, I take it you can hear me?"

"I can indeed. I take it you enjoyed my little game?"

"About as much as a trip to the dentist," Hawke said. "Who is this?"

"You can call me the Director."

Les said, "Just what the hell is the point of all this?"

"The point is twofold," the voice said. "First, to slow you down and get you off the beaten track, slowing you down in your pursuit of me and finding the real Shangri

La, the second was a wonderful opportunity to blow the three of you to pieces with my AI-controlled machine guns. It looks like they might require some sort of improvement, considering two of you are fit and well and one was only partially wounded. This is disappointing."

"That takes a pretty twisted mind," Lea said.

As she spoke, Hawke noticed something next to his boot, something small and shiny that was glittering among the pile of shattered glass lying all over the floor. He leaned forward, picked it up and slid it inside a pocket on his combat vest.

"If you think that was twisted, wait until you see what I've got in store for the rest of the world. Anyway, I must go. I have many important things to do, so don't think me too rude when I say goodbye. You may have got through the machine guns but you certainly won't get past the Semtex. Goodbye, Joe Hawke and Lea Donovan. Forever."

Hawke and Lea didn't need to say anything. They both leapt up to their feet and Lea ran to the door. Hawke screamed at her, asking her where she was going.

"I'm getting down the stairs, that is where I'm going!" Lea yelled.

"There's no time for that!" Hawke said. "He wouldn't give us a head start like that! Quick through the window."

Hawke sprayed the office's outside window with machine gun bullets, blasting every last shard of glass out of the frame. Then they dived head-first out of the window, just as the plastic explosives inside the warehouse detonated. The explosion was ferocious, buckling the steel walls behind them and sending an enormous fireball out through the window in their wake, each of them feeling the fierce heat of the billowing smoke and debris blasting out behind them on their backs. They both tumbled down towards the dumpsters below the office window, crashing into an enormous pile of garbage.

"And that's why we always do a reconnoitre of the property before we storm it," Hawke said, picking a rotten banana skin off his shoulder and throwing it into the bin behind him.

With debris still raining down on their heads. Lea cursed. "This absolutely bloody stinks!"

"Better than being in there," Hawke said, nodding his head to indicate up in the office.

He climbed up out of the heap, then helped Lea as she clambered through it and landed with a soft thump in the snow beside him. Then the two of them ran around the side of the warehouse and joined up with Ryan who was still concealed behind the dumpsters on the other side of the yard.

"Just what the hell happened?" Ryan asked.

Hawke and Lea turned and looked at the warehouse, dwarfed by a two-hundred-foot-high fireball billowing up into the sky.

"I think we need to talk about that somewhere else," Hawke said. "Because something tells me this place is going to get very busy, very soon."

"And that somewhere else had better be a hospital," Lea said, taking in Ryan's leg. "So let's get moving."

CHAPTER THIRTY

Licking their wounds in a motel close to JFK Airport, most of the ECHO team were now gathered together, eating takeaway pizza and drinking chilled coke from one of the vending machines outside the front office.

"Hawke took a long swig of the coke and then set his bottle down on the window sill before turning around and stretching his arms and giving a long yawn.

"You seem very relaxed, considering just how much we screwed up this entire mission," Scarlet said.

"That's because I think we have a clue."

Everyone in the team turned to face him. Lea spoke first.

"What do you mean we have a clue? What we've got is a lot of cuts and bruises and one man down, currently sitting in the nearest hospital getting his leg put back together again."

"Ryan's with Reaper. He'll be fine," Scarlet said.

Hawke checked his watch. "Talking of which, they should both be getting back soon, shouldn't they? Have either of them given us a call?"

Scarlet shook her head. "No, but I know Vincent and he'll call just as soon as he's ready to call and not a moment before. If he hasn't called, it just means they're still sitting in hospital getting Ryan's leg put back together, as Lea put it so quaintly."

"I was going to give this little treat to Ryan," Hawke said, "But as selfish bastard clearly has more important things to do, I'll give it to you instead, Alex."

Hawke pulled the small shiny object he had found on the office floor back at the warehouse from his combat vest and threw it in Alex's general direction.

The young American woman reached out and caught it without flinching, then she brought her closed fist down in front of her face and opened it to see what she had just caught. A wide smile spread on her face and she looked up a Hawke, her eyes sparkling with hope.

"Is this what I think it is?"

The others were now leaning around her, craning their necks and trying to see what he had thrown at her.

"If you think it's a sim card, then you're right," Hawke said.

"I know it's a sim card, Joe," Alex said with a roll of her eyes. "What I meant was, did you find it back at the warehouse?"

"What do you think?" Hawke said, reaching down and snatching a big fat slice of pepperoni pizza from the greasy box on the bed.

"For God's sake, don't put the box on the bed," Lea said. "How many times have I told you those things leave a grease stain?"

"Yeah, I don't think we're all that bothered about grease stains right now," Scarlet said.

"Well, you should be because someone's got to clean that up," Lea said. "Besides that, we'll lose our deposit."

Kahlia and Ravi burst into laughter, neither of them sure whether Lea was making a joke or not. Before either of them had got to the bottom of it, Hawke replied to Alex.

"Yes, I found the SIM card back in the warehouse," he explained.

"And you didn't say anything to me about it," Lea said. "I thought we were supposed to be partners – in every sense of the word."

"The funny thing is, at the time I was being peppered with machine gun bullets and I'd just been told by a psychopath that the entire building was about to explode, courtesy of an inordinate quantity of plastic explosives packed all around me. When I saw it on the floor, I just picked it up and chucked it in my vest. I promised myself that I would tell you just as soon as I could and then I forgot about it. What are you gonna do?"

"None of that's important," Scarlet said. "What's important is that we have a potential clue."

"We might have absolutely nothing," Kahlia said, momentarily bringing the mood down. "It's just a sim card that you found on the floor of a warehouse office space somewhere. There could have been endless people in and out of there since those psychopaths moved out."

"We should hire you out for children's parties," Scarlet said. "You really know how to lift the mood of a room."

"I agree with Scarlet," Lea said. "I'd much rather take a positive view of this if it's all right with everybody else.

What do you think Alex? Is there some way we could find out anything from it?"

Alex was already tapping away on her mobile phone. "Of course there is," she said. "Getting information out of it in terms of digital information may be a problem if it's badly damaged, but we'll find out about that soon enough. In the meantime, I can already tell you that it has an Icelandic country code printed on it."

Ravi leaned in. "How can you tell?"

"It's embossed right here on the integrated circuit of the SIM card," Alex said. "Look on the plastic frame of the sim card. Do you see these numbers +354? That's the country code for Iceland."

"And you know that right off the top of your head?" Kahlia asked, clearly impressed.

"Are you freaking kidding me? I just looked it up while you were all arguing about whether SIM cards could be of any use or not."

Alex was already powering down her phone and taking off the back cover, taking out her own sim card and inserting the new one into the sim card tray. She powered her phone back up and was relieved to see that it was not pin code enabled. "There's not a lot of data here, it looks like it's been corrupted in some way."

A gloomy sigh of frustration went around the room.

"Is there any GPS data on there?" Lea asked.

"It's extremely unlikely there's any GPS data on here," Alex said. "The GPS capabilities would have been part of the phone, not the sim card. Wait – what's this?"

Alex's eyebrows rose an inch on her forehead and everyone gathered in even closer around her.

"What have you got?" Hawke asked, still chewing hungrily on the big slice of pepperoni pizza.

"When I inserted the sim card into my phone, it seems to have activated some kind of bespoke application that I'm not familiar with. It looks like this application was probably developed by the mercenaries to track the telephone that the sim card was originally in."

Hawke shrugged. "They probably do it to all of their operatives."

"Why not just use the regular native GPS features on the telephone?" Ravi asked.

Alex replied. "It looks like a separate, bespoke application that is designed to run in the background, hidden from the user of the phone. Clearly whoever's in charge of these guys doesn't trust any of his operatives."

"You mean they might turn off the GPS data native to the phone, but they'd still be able to be tracked by whoever put this app on the sim card?" Kahlia asked.

"I mean exactly that," Alex said, furiously working on her phone. "I've been able to reverse engineer this data trail and I can tell you that this phone has pretty much only been in two locations since it was switched on. One is right here in New York City and the other is in a completely deserted part of northern Iceland."

"Northern Iceland?" Scarlet said. "Whereabouts exactly?"

Alex held up the phone for everyone else to see. Hawke was particularly interested to see the large cluster of little red dots, representing the various GPS locations the telephone's user had been in while in Iceland. It was a completely unpopulated part of the north of the island and looked like it was covered in snow, many miles from the nearest town.

He swallowed his pizza. "Looks like we just found the real Shangri La," he said.

THE MIDNIGHT SYNDICATE

*

The night flight into the Arctic was tense and nasty. Heavy turbulence pounded them for hundreds of miles, and the blackness outside the aircraft only increased their sense of uneasiness as they raced towards their final destination.

At least they were together again, Hawke considered. The successful rescue of Ravi and Kahlia meant the full complement of ECHO was now preparing to attack the real Shangri La, and the Director's efforts to divide them had failed. Ryan's leg was dressed properly and he was pumped with painkillers. There would be no more fieldwork for him, but he could hang back and work the tech, just like in the old days. Maybe things were looking up, the old Marine thought to himself. He yawned and stretched out in his seat. He had tried to get some sleep, as was his habit on most flights, but tonight he was unable to, and instead spent his time thinking about if he and Lea would leave ECHO or not. Sometimes this seemed like a good idea to him, other times he wasn't so sure. Something told him the next few hours might help him make up his mind.

CHAPTER THIRTY-ONE

The Director stared out of his window, which gave a view of the enormous Icelandic ice cave inside which they had built Shangri La. From here he was able to look out on a bizarre but beautiful world of strange ice formations stretching out in front of him as if he were inside some kind of depraved jaw. A mysterious bluish glow shimmered over it all. The source was an unspecified bioluminescent organism they had discovered down in the uncharted cave while digging out the foundations for the control compound.

He heard something they had still not grown used to – a deep eerie creaking sound coming from the rocks surrounding the cave. He told himself it was merely a geographical feature, no matter how much it sounded like some awful living thing stalking him from the black depths beyond. It was unnerving, but a dark part of him enjoyed it.

At least his plan was coming together. Hawke and Lea were blown to smithereens in the warehouse explosion and if Ryan Bale managed somehow to escape the explosion he was badly wounded and bleeding out on the car park floor. Excellent. This was enough to be going on with, especially as he had significantly bigger fish to fry with what was unfolding all around him. Compared to his plans, the ECHO team were no more than an annoying nuisance, the proverbial thorn in his side.

Zarina approached from his right and walked across to him, pausing to stand on her tiptoes and kiss him on the cheek before walking casually over to the drinks cabinet and pouring herself a generous Courvoisier brandy.

"Would you like one, my darling?" she purred.

He turned to admire the blonde Russian beauty. He knew it was his power that attracted her to him, but he didn't care. She was his, no matter what the motive. "Not at all," he said coolly. "I have far too much on my mind. My plans demand constant concentration and total focus. Brandy would only dull my most essential faculties. Besides I must now talk to the Syndicate. They have gathered in the briefing room next door and it is time they learned the full truth of my plans. Will you join me?"

The Director and Zarina strolled across his study and slid open two large, heavy walnut doors which brushed gently on their runners to reveal a large corporate conference room. The people making up the Midnight Syndicate sat around a large table and turned their faces to him and the Russian woman standing at his side. She took a long sip of the brandy and walked over to one of the empty seats. As she sat down, the Director moved around to the head of the table, but instead of sitting down, he pushed his chair in and remained standing behind it.

"Ladies and gentlemen, thank you for gathering here today. You are representatives of all of the most adept and criminal cyber mercenary organisations on the planet and your presence here is greatly appreciated. Today, we are gathered here for an important and unique reason, a life-changing, world-altering reason. We are all very happy to be here, I know. I for one have waited my entire life for an opportunity like this."

He now addressed the AI. "Crucible, please begin the presentation."

The wall behind him now retracted to reveal a large plasma screen the full size of the wall, at least ten feet high and twenty feet across. It felt more like being in a private cinema than watching a regular presentation. Now on the screen, an image of New York City appeared. The Director knew everyone presumed the images were taken by a drone, but soon they would be disabused of that notion and realise that like most of the things he was connected to, they were watching nothing less than an AI representation of the city. That would be clear enough in just a few seconds.

A voice began to speak. It was a woman's voice, cool and calm and collected. She had a refined Newport accent and spoke with an engaging and professional inflexion. Like the images of the city they were watching, she too was nothing less than an AI.

"New York City," the voice began. "Home to over eight million people, this world-famous city, constituted of its five boroughs: Manhattan, Brooklyn, Queens, the Bronx and Staten Island, is one of the world's most visited cities, as well as being one of the world's greatest and most powerful financial hubs."

As the cool voice narrated the video, the camera now closed in on the New York Stock Exchange.

She began talking again. "Founded in 1792 when just twenty-four merchants and stockbrokers signed what is now known as the Buttonwood Agreement – named so because it was signed under a buttonwood tree on Wall Street – the New York Stock Exchange is the oldest stock exchange in the United States and considered to be one of the most prestigious and important financial institutions in the entire world. Inside these hallowed walls, the average day might see the Exchange handle anywhere from a few hundred billion dollars to well over a trillion US dollars in various trades. Not only does this make it a financial hub, but it makes it a security hub. If the New York Stock Exchange were to suffer some kind of fatal attack, this would have a devastating effect on world stability and security and chaos would ripple around the planet within hours."

The Director watched the faces of those gathered around the conference table as the AI simulation rapidly turned into abject horror. First, there was a simulation of all the power going down across the exchange and the ensuing chaos, then a swarm of AI drones appeared around the roof of the stock exchange and launched missiles into the building. As the exchange exploded in a massive fireball, the image faded and went quiet. The Director now turned and addressed the Midnight Syndicate once again.

"You see ladies and gentlemen, with my AI programme, I can completely control every single location on Earth that has used any kind of digital technology. Water infrastructure, the electricity grid, food distribution, food growing, the manufacturing base, the healthcare sector, top secret military installations – you name it and I will have full control over it. Not only will I easily take control of it, but I also have the option to destroy it at any time I desire, all because of the unassailable power of this new, proprietary AI system known as the Crucible. Between us, we can deploy this all over the world and use local resources to adapt to any attack made against us."

A murmur of excitement rippled around the members of the Midnight Syndicate. The possibilities were infinite.

"When can this go ahead?" one of them asked.

The Director smiled. "Within a few hours, world leaders will be begging for my mercy and then we will dictate terms. There is nothing – and I mean absolutely nothing that can stop us now."

CHAPTER THIRTY-TWO

Night hung heavily and rose slowly over Iceland's Tröllaskagi Peninsula as their jet landed at the Siglufjörður Airport on the southern side of the bay. This was a wild land of fjords and rugged snowcapped mountains and even the view from the airport was breathtaking as they taxied to a gentle stop just in front of the tiny airport. It was already past midday and at this time of year, the sun would only creep up above the horizon for a very short time before sinking back down again for another twenty-hour-long night.

ECHO had been lucky with the landing, but now the weather was beginning to close in once again, as they had expected after studying the radar maps of northern Iceland on the flight over from New York City. As they climbed out of the small jet, Lea looked up into the sky and shivered, pulling her collar up around her neck for warmth. The sky was divided into two perfect hemispheres. The western half was a wild black vault scattered with piercingly bright white stars and a mesmerising green curtain of northern lights flickering and dancing above the world, like spirits from an ancient time. The eastern half was covered by a thick blanket of snow clouds that were gradually swallowing up the stars second by second. Behind the airport rose a snowy mountain, rising on the peninsula they had just flown over before landing. Ahead of them, just in front of the airport was a long, sleek snowmobile trailer hooked up to a Toyota Hilux.

"Hope everyone brought their thermal socks," Hawke said, his breath pluming in a thick cloud in front of his face. "Because it looks like it's gonna get a bit nippy from here on in."

"My trailer was stocked with Arctic provisions before you left New York," said a man walking towards them from the Hilux.

"Kristjan!" Reaper said. "My old comrade in arms."

"I wouldn't exactly put it like that," the man said, shaking Reaper warmly with his gloved hand. "But it's great to see you. I couldn't believe it when I got your message. I got everything you asked for."

"So this is Kristjan," Scarlet said. "Vincent's told me a lot about your time together in the French Foreign Legion."

"All good, I hope." He turned to the rest of the team. "I'm Kristjan Sigurdsson. I worked with Vincent in the Legion for many years. Good times."

As they talked, Kristjan walked them over to his trailer and opened it up. "Et voila! It's all here – insulated Parkas, high-traction boots, balaclavas, GPS devices, some ice axes and snow shovels, a first aid kit, flares, some PDWs – FN P90s and HK MP5s – a Barrett M82 sniper rifle... you name it."

Hawke who had trained in the Royal Marine Commandos Arctic and Mountain Warfare Cadre looked almost disappointed. Looking at the retired Icelandic soldier, he said, "Don't make it too easy for me, Kristjan!"

"And you're sure this place is in some sort of cave?" Lea asked.

Kristjan nodded. "Definitely. I've been over there a thousand times. There's nowhere other than an ice cave in which to hide any kind of covert compound. Do you have the exact coordinates?"

She gave them to him.

"Yes, that area is riddled with blue glacier caves."

"How long do you think it will take us to reach the entrance to the cave?" Lea asked Kristjan.

"Not too long," the Icelander said, looking up at the sky and surveying the weather. "In these conditions, we'll be there in less than an hour. I know the area well and some ways are quicker than others."

"That's why you're here, darling," Scarlet said, giving the tall blond man a wink.

"It's like I'm not even here," Reaper said with a laugh.

Hawke poked his head inside the trailer. "Are the snowmobiles already loaded up?"

"Not yet, you can do it on the drive up there."

They continued talking as they stepped into the trailer. "Thanks for this, Kristjan," Lea said. "I'm not going to ask where it all came from."

"Please don't."

Hawke hefted a canister of grenades up from the trailer floor onto the back of one of the snowmobiles. Glancing at the rest of the equipment and provisions that had been supplied by the Icelander, he quietly harboured some doubts they had enough weapons for the job, but that depended entirely upon the size of the Director's forces when they reached the cave system.

"Let's just hope we can get there in time," Alex said. "We don't know much about this Crucible, but whatever it is, it's got to be more than a match for these weapons – no offence, Kristjan."

"None taken. What do you think this Crucible weapon might be? Some kind of EMP device, maybe?"

"Maybe," Alex said. "But I think an AI system is closer to the mark. If so, they could cripple much of our tech."

"Well, they haven't done it yet," Ryan said, wincing in pain as he hobbled across to the trailer on two crutches. "We had no problem with any of the GPS Tech on board the plane or with our phones. Internet's up and running in the normal way. I'm pretty sure that will be the first thing these bastards take down if they can because that's going to create the most chaos. After that, it'll be water treatment plants and nuclear power stations."

"You always know how to cheer me up, Ryan," Alex said. "How's the leg?"

"Not too bad. I still think I can use a gun."

"Don't be ridiculous," Lea said. "You're staying back with Kristjan until it's all over."

Ryan gave her a mock, two-finger salute.

Having finished packing the snowmobiles, they bade farewell to John Richardson, the pilot Sir Richard Eden had arranged to get them to Iceland. He disappeared into the airport, with instructions to wait until the mission was over and then return them to Elysium. Hawke made one final survey of the frozen bay. A blast of icy Arctic air cut across his face and he pulled up his Parker coat over his head, pulling the zip up to its maximum height. Like everyone else, he was only too happy to slip on his thick Arctic gloves. Everyone seemed to be holding up fairly well although Kahlia looked like she would sooner be anywhere else than here.

The rest of the team climbed into the Hilux and the snowmobile trailer and began the short journey up the peninsula. No one spoke much on the journey, until they got a message from Eden, confirming that the Crucible was indeed an advanced AI capable of creating practically limitless carnage on the world. When they arrived at the small town of Hofsós, it was time to transfer to a boat, hastily arranged by Kristjan. They swiftly took the fully-packed snowmobiles out of the trailer and bid farewell to Kristjan and Ryan, who would be staying out of the way in this part of the peninsula.

"Take care," Ryan said to Alex, then kissed her, eliciting a wolf whistle from Scarlet.

Behind her back, Alex gave the Englishwoman her middle finger, causing a few nervous chuckles.

"Okay everyone," Hawke said. "We all read the message from Rich. We can't have many hours left until these guys can put the Crucible online and then the entire planet becomes no more than their plaything. If they want to, they will be able to kill hundreds of millions of people by cutting off water from power stations, overloading nuclear power stations, and bypassing security systems around the world, including those in maximum security prisons. They'll be able to compromise worldwide cryptographic systems, triggering a total breakdown of supposedly secure communications and transactions around the world, and of course, they'll immediately unleash endless smaller cyber-attacks all over the planet. They'll also have total control of power grids, transportation systems and water supplies and they'll be empowered to trigger massive outages, disruptions or total failures."

Hawke continued to glance over the list of possible destruction Eden had included in his latest communiqué to them. "According to this, they'll be able to power down hospitals and hack into medical records and AI-lead diagnostic systems and treatment protocols, leading to all manner of chaos and horrors in the healthcare systems of the world. It can solve any encryption. It's a major game changer.

"Pretty damned smart though," Alex said.

"Whether you think it's clever or not is irrelevant, but the truth is, nearly everyone in the world is completely dependent on AI and digital computer systems for nearly everything in their lives. Once the Director has the Crucible online, he rules the world and we're the only ones who can stop it."

When he finished speaking he climbed onto his snowmobile, fired it up and navigated over onto the gangplank leading up to the boat bobbing up and down in the small harbour. The water here was extremely cold and beginning to ice around the edges of the port. They were lucky that it wasn't frozen because this boat, the 'Aurora', was no icebreaker.

When the snowmobiles were safely aboard the Aurora everyone except Hawke and Lea went inside the cabin and below decks to warm up. Hawke decided to stand on the stern of the boat and watch Kristjan and Ryan and the loading point gradually disappear into the darkness as they sailed out of the port. It was a dangerous journey, but a temporary road closure caused by a snowstorm left them with little choice. Kristjan's quick thinking and local contacts had saved the day, and now they would round the peninsula this way instead.

Lea saw Hawke and walked over to give him some company, like him, she was protected in full Arctic warfare gear, including a thick Parka, zipped up to the top and some good, thick white gloves.

"That was some speech you gave back there, Josiah. I didn't think you had it in ya."

"I don't know what it is about this mission Lea," Hawke said. "But there's something about it that bothers me. It's not just how idiotic it is for people to have developed systems that are this vulnerable to destruction by malicious actors like the Director, but I just can't get the Order of the Black Wolf out of my mind. When Scorpion told me that they were trying to steal Poseidon's Trident, I got a very bad feeling."

"What are you saying?"

"I think she's wrapped up in this somehow?"

"What, you think she's the Director of the Midnight Syndicate?"

"Maybe. I just wondered if she's playing a part in this somewhere. It could be her."

"Well, I don't think she's the Director, Joe."

"Why hasn't she attacked us? Why hasn't she attacked anywhere? Our surveillance systems would have picked up any enemy action made by her and yet we've heard nothing at all. It's not like Richard has contacted us and told us that the Order of the Black Wolf has launched an attack somewhere and we have to respond to that in some way. I just don't like the way her name popped up and then disappeared again. It puts me on edge."

"One problem at a time, Joe," Lea said. "Don't go meeting trouble halfway, you know what I mean? Maybe Helga Bloody Zaugg is full of shit, just like her father. For now, you need to stay focused on the Director and the Midnight Syndicate, we all do. Everything you said in your little speech to the troops back there is completely true and that's probably only the half of it. You can't be thinking about Helga Zaugg at a time like this."

"I know... and I'm not," he said reassuringly. "I'm just saying that I know she's out there somewhere. It just feels like we're waiting for a trap to spring."

"C'mon," she said, wrapping her arm around his and pulling him away from the stern. "Let's get down inside. They said they were going to make some coffee. Won't be long before we're out on the snowmobiles."

Hawke followed Lea down the port side of the boat to the cabin and then stepped inside behind her. The cabin was not exactly warm, but several degrees warmer than outside, so he unzipped his Parka hood and pulled it down off of his head as they walked down below decks. By the time he had taken his gloves off, Alex had poured everyone a large mug of steaming, milky coffee and there was even a packet of biscuits, helpfully supplied by Kristjan in anticipation of their energy needs.

Hawke sat down at the table with his friends, drank coffee and ate biscuits and enjoyed the sensation of the boat rolling and pitching gently. As a man with much experience on the water, he knew this meant they had now left the little port and were turning northeast towards their final destination.

Scarlet Sloane raised a coffee mug into the air and proposed a toast.

"To the bastard Director and his army of arseholes crashing and burning tonight!"

Hawke couldn't have said it any better himself, and as he raised his mug into the toast, he felt fully on the job ahead of him.

Zaugg could wait.

CHAPTER THIRTY-THREE

The Director stood at the very heart of his inner sanctum. All around him, on dozens of CCTV screens and computer monitors, an endless blizzard of information was bombarding his mind. Taking a moment to himself to gather his thoughts before initiating the final phase of the plan, he stared up into the giant space above the busy control room and then closed his eyes and reminded himself that what he was doing today was the best for humanity. Opening his eyes, he focused now on the faces of the twenty-five men and women on the large bank of plasma monitors on the control room's wall.

These were the leaders of the G20 countries and the five leaders of the BRICS countries were directly beneath them. The faces of these men and women were not the usual confident ones seen by the members of the public on the television set and handheld devices, but the terrified, ashen faces of men and women stricken with terror. For one thing, these were the people who summoned others to come to them, and the Director knew only too well the effect of his summoning them to appear before him would have had on their psychologies. For another thing, by now they already knew of the extreme power he was about to wield and they also would know that none of them could do anything about it. They were entirely vulnerable to his mercy. He liked that. He was enjoying the power, as he knew he would.

He turned to a man sitting just to his right, attending to one of the monitors. "What's going on with our uninvited guests on the snowmobiles?"

"They're making their way up the western slope, sir. There appears to be less of them and they don't look particularly well-armed."

The Director followed them on his CCTV screen as they ploughed across the snowfield, rooster tails of snow flying off the spike snow tyres behind them. "Bale was wounded back in New York, that is why there are less of them. But, don't ever be complacent with a man like Joe Hawke. I've seen him in action more than once and you've also seen him at work back in the warehouse in Manhattan. I'm not in any way comforted by the fact that we outnumber them and outgun them, at least not yet. Are the Cayman Crew here yet?"

"Yes, they arrived recently."

"Good, they'll be needed," the Director said. "I need to see some kind of proof that we're getting on top of ECHO before I can think of relaxing. Either way, you can see that I have some important business to attend to, make sure Hawke and the rest of the ECHO team get nowhere near this facility. You know what failure will mean and this time I will deal with you personally."

"Yes, sir," the man said. He immediately turned and began barking orders into the Lavalier wearable microphone positioned an inch in front of his mouth. Leaving the matter firmly to his young assistant, the Director now turned his attention to the bank of plasma screens up on the far wall where the world's most powerful people were impatiently waiting for him to begin.

"Good evening, ladies and gentlemen," the Director began. "I trust you can all hear me properly because this is not something I want to say more than once." He waited a few seconds to ensure that every one of the leaders was having the information relayed to them in good time and translated properly. When he could see that his words were reaching all of the men and women assembled before him, he glanced at Zarina off to his right and when she smiled back, giving him a renewed boost of confidence, he continued with his little speech.

"You are assembled here today before me, charged with crimes against humanity. The Midnight Syndicate has found you guilty and you are now to be given your punishments. You are of course wondering why a man like me could have the power to accuse you of such a heinous crime or indeed to threaten you with punishment for what you have done, but by now I believe I have given you a sure enough sign of the power at my command and the very fact that you are all here now appearing before me shows me that you take that seriously. That is what gives me the power to accuse you of crimes against humanity and that is what gives me the power to mete out any punishment I so desire."

As his words were being translated and comprehended by the shocked leaders of the world's most powerful countries right in front of him, he felt Zarina's hand wrap around his own at his side.

"This is outrageous!" barked the British Prime Minister. "How dare you speak to us like this?"

The Director was about to respond when he heard a long string of German, a language incomprehensible to him, so he waited for the translation. This was done automatically by his AI system and now he heard the German's words translated into English, just a fraction of a second behind the original German.

"I quite agree with the British Prime Minister. This is an outrage! You have no right to summon us here and speak to us like this. The German Government will not accept any of these so-called punishments and neither will accede to any demand made here today."

"I have every right!" the Director snapped. "The right is given to me by my total power!" He screamed this at the top of his voice, making every man and woman on the plasma screens recoil with horror. Perhaps he thought they were in awe of his power, but more likely they were terrified by how deranged he had become and also how quickly. "The AI at my fingertips gives me the raw power to do anything I please and to talk to any of you in any way I wish!"

He felt Zarina's hand slip away from his own as she took a step off to the right. It didn't bother him; he knew only too well how much she disliked or even feared his notorious tempers. It mattered nothing at all because all that mattered was how hard he could hammer home his message to these ignorant men and women before him with their dangerous mix of ignorance and arrogance, that he was now in power. Not them.

The American president was now speaking. "We don't know exactly who you are or exactly what you want, but we do know that you're not gonna get it. I've already spoken with my Joint Chiefs of Staff and my National Security Adviser, along with several other officials in the Oval Office this afternoon and I've made private telephone calls to the other world leaders and — "

The Director cut him off immediately. "Don't waste your breath, Mr President. Every single one of the telephone calls that you made to other world leaders, the ones you believed were heavily encrypted, were all immediately hacked and translated by my AI system in real-time. I've also already read transcripts of all of the telephone conversations you held with all of the other members of the Five Eyes Security Alliance. I know everything you've planned and I have already taken steps to thwart all of your retaliation plans."

The look on the president's face alone was now worth all of the trouble he had gone to over the last few years. None of them had expected this. But they should have, this was one of the things that made him angrier than anything. They weren't taking him or his threats seriously. Perhaps now they would.

"I don't believe you," the president said.

"Nice try, Mr President… and I do respect your quite passable acting technique, but we both know that you *do* believe me and if you don't, perhaps this will change your mind. I already know about the USS *Arizona* and the Russian submarine, *Vladimir Monomakh*, both of which are now approaching Iceland, one from the southwest and one from the northeast. I know about your plans to fire small-scale nuclear weapons at my facility here, with the agreement of your NATO partners in Reykjavík, and my AI system has already taken steps to ensure that this doesn't happen. First, those submarines are already nowhere near where they think they are, and second, if they fire those missiles they will be instantly redirected to Washington DC and Moscow. We have the power to do so and I'm tired of having to prove myself, but if I have to prove myself one more time to make you understand, then perhaps let me do this."

The Director now turned to Zarina. She looked like she had calmed down a little since his earlier outburst but was still keeping her distance. He fixed her in the eye. "Zarina, pick a random city in the United States."

She mulled the matter over for a few seconds and the Director enjoyed watching the enraged, frustrated expressions on the faces of the world leaders in front of him. Eventually, in a calm and amused tone, Zarina gave him her randomly selected city. "Dallas."

"Any particular reason?" The Director asked. It wasn't just for his amusement, but he was giving the AI time to work its magic. It would take only a few seconds anyway, but it would look better if it was instantaneous. Ever the showman.

Zarina shrugged. "I just watched the TV show once. I enjoyed it."

"Crucible!" the Director said out loud. "Cut all power and water services to Dallas."

The world leaders sat in silence, each in their own respective office and none of them were sure how to react.

The Italian Prime Minister even chuckled a little before saying something. Once again it was instantly translated by the AI and pumped through the speakers in the control room: "This is nonsense!" he said. "Why are we wasting our time with this fool?"

The Director wasn't watching him and he wasn't listening to him. His eyes were fixed on the American president, whose face he now saw drop as his eyes wandered off-screen. He was looking at somebody behind the camera in the Oval Office. And the Director knew why. The American president now fixed his eyes on the camera and addressed the Director once again. "Dallas just lost all its power and its water services have been cut off. I demand that you return these services!"

"Do you take me seriously now?"

"Yes, I take you seriously. Now turn that power back on!"

"What do you think, Zarina?" the Director said. He was playing the same trick as before, giving the AI a few seconds to evade all of the security in the Texan city's electricity and water infrastructure.

"Yes you can turn it on," she purred. "The television programme was not so bad.

The Director addressed the AI. "Crucible, return all power and water to Dallas."

He now saw the president look off camera once again, give a brief angry nod and then return his attention to the camera. Before he could speak, the Director said: "So, now when I tell you those submarines are nowhere near where they think they are and that if they fire their payloads – the ones aimed at us – they will be redirected and delivered in glorious form to Washington DC and Moscow, do I take it you believe me?"

The Russian president spoke angrily, his words again being instantly translated into English by the AI. "Yes, we believe you."

The American president nodded. "I'm listening. Go ahead."

"Good, because what I have to say is going to shock you to your core."

CHAPTER THIRTY-FOUR

With the Northern Lights still shimmering above their heads, Lea smiled at Hawke and climbed off her snowmobile. "Who's at the back?" she asked, looking down the hill at the remaining snowmobiles that were still driving up towards them.

"I think that's Ravi and Kalia, but I'm not sure," he said, watching the lights of the trailing snowmobiles lancing the snowstorm like needles.

Scarlet skidded to a halt beside them, throwing a high arc of powdery snow into the air behind her. She removed her helmet and swore. "I want my palm trees back."

When they were all present, they left the snowmobiles and trekked up the slope to a crest which overlooked the blue glacier caves hiding the compound. It was a short but tough slog, and when they reached the top, they crashed down in the snow and took a moment to get their breath back.

Hawke shivered as the biting winds of northern Iceland cut across the exposed part of his face and underscored all over again why Richard Eden had chosen to base ECHO's control compound in the Caribbean and not somewhere in the Arctic Circle. It also reminded him of his earlier days in the military.

They were good happy days, but he didn't want to return to them any time soon – plus he was nearly three decades older than when he had done that training and didn't fancy his chances this time around. Glancing down to the bottom of the slope where they had left the snowmobiles, he saw the snowfall had already covered their tracks. Further out, the Aurora was sheltering in a cove, not visible from the bottom of the valley where the compound was located.

"What do you think?" he said to Scarlet. She was lying at his side and staring through the binoculars he had just handed her at the compound below in the valley.

"I think it's suspiciously quiet," Scarlet said. "That's what I think. I also think I'm too bloody old to be doing this."

"Just think of it as service to King and Country," Hawke said.

"He's not my bloody king," Lea said in her Irish lilt. "So, who the hell am I doing it for? Not the bloody Irish president, that's for damn sure."

"We all know what Rich would say," Alex said. "ECHO floats above all of these countries and loyalties. We do this for the world."

Scarlet looked at her with something approaching nausea on her face. "Pass me a sick bag. I don't do this for world peace. I do it for the challenge and I do it because I like taking scumbags like the Cayman Crew out of the equation. I do it because it pays the best and I want to buy my private island one day. So you can stick world peace right up there where the sun doesn't shine."

"You see I try to instil a sense of decency and honour in her," Alex said, "but she just throws it back in my face."

Behind them, Ravi was chuckling. Reaper was staring through the binoculars giving the site below his own particular brand of analysis and attention.

"What do you see, Reap?" Alex asked. Like the rest of them, she was now lying on the crest of a snowy ridge to the compound's west, pushed down deep into the snow with barely a few inches at the top of their heads showing as they surveyed the compound.

"I think that calling it Shangri La was a bit of a joke," Reaper said. "This is about as far from my images of Shangri La as it's possible to get."

"Couldn't agree more friend," Hawke said, taking the binoculars back off him and this time tracking away from the compound up to the ridge on the other side of the valley. "I think there's a small watch team up there, too."

The binoculars were infrared and able to make out body heat. Hawke was now looking at the heat signatures of three adults up on the far ridge who were not taking particular care in disguising themselves.

"Give us the binoculars," Lea said, taking them from him. She looked on the same section of the ridge opposite them on the far side of the valley, where Hawke had seen the figures and agreed with his view that three figures were nestling in what looked like a temporary snow structure. "A little bit obvious, isn't it?"

Hawke nodded. "Yes, far too obvious. I find it difficult to believe a compound like this has only got three soldiers defending it. They're on watch, but why so obvious?

Whatever the reason is, we're not gonna let them take too much of our attention."

"Do you think they've seen us?" Kahlia asked.

"Not since I've been staring at them with the infrared binoculars," Hawke said. "Because they're not looking back at us with any binoculars or any other type of assisted night vision. Not to say they didn't catch us as soon as we pulled up here. We did keep a pretty low profile as we crept up to the crest of the hill, so I'm thinking we're clear."

Lea gazed across the moonlit snowfield as the northern lights continued to dance and flicker above her head. From her perspective, it was an eerie, silvery landscape, abruptly ending where the black sky began. It reminded her of the pictures she had seen of Apollo astronauts on the moon. It was beauty like this that reminded her why she did what she did and convinced her that the risks she took every day would always be worth it.

Hawke shifted across and pulled up alongside her and cut the engine. Brushing the snow off his face and gloves, he cursed and turned to her. "What a godforsaken dump."

"So, what's the plan?" Kahlia said.

"The plan is we go down there, break into that place and take out as many of those bastards as we can," Hawke said. "And then when we've done that, we shut down that goddam Crucible creation and return humanity to itself."

"You make that sound very easy," Alex said sarcastically.

"It's not gonna be easy," Hawke said, "and I didn't mean to make it sound easy. We're gonna break into three and we're gonna storm the compound in the old-fashioned style, giving them two fronts to deal with."

"Sorry if my maths is failing me here, Josiah," Lea said, but I thought you said we were going to break into three?"

"I did," Hawke said.

"But you just said we were going to attack him on two fronts."

"Yes, that's right," Hawke said insistently. "We're going to attack them on two fronts."

"So why are we splitting into three?" Lea asked again.

"Because I'm going to go down there quietly ahead of the main battle and get inside so I can be the enemy within, that sort of thing. You know, a bit of commando derring-do. Plant an explosive treat for later, and so on."

Lea rolled her eyes. "And just how the hell are you going to go inside on your own?"

Hawke handed her his monocular. "Take another gander down there. If you look at the compound with the thermal imaging monocular, you'll see a heat signature at the back of the compound on the northeastern corner. This is either an exhaust fan or an air intake opening for a surface intake ventilation system. An easier way in than the main entrance."

He took the monocular from her and stuffed it in his combat vest.

"And as the saying goes: what goes in must come out, he said. "But in this case the system that lets that hot air out is gonna let me in. All good?"

"Sounds dangerous," Kahlia said.

Hawke gave her a look. "Everything we do is dangerous. You're about to charge into battle through a snowfield and fight an unknown enemy in open Arctic combat. That sounds dangerous too, doesn't it?"

Kahlia shrugged. "When you put it like that…"

The rest of the team smiled as they prepared to make their move.

"Who else has got a thermal imaging monocular?" Hawke asked.

"I have," Reaper said patting his combat vest.

"Good, then you can watch me go all the way down there and when you see me disappear through that vent, that's when you break into two and start the attack. But first, we have some business to take care of."

He reached down into his pack and keeping his head below the ridgeline, he pulled out the sniper Kristjan had provided and set it up, screwing the muffler on and loading it, then he pull a round into the chamber and aimed at the three men opposite on the far ridge. He squeezed the trigger once. Twice. Three times. Three shots in one second. The sound was muffled by the silencer on the end of the barrel and all three men slumped out of view another second later.

"They wouldn't have had time even to know what happened," Hawke said. "Let alone make a radio call. I don't know why the hell they were there, but they're gone now. Had to kill them. There was no other way I could get down to the compound without them radioing my presence in. That must have been their purpose. All right everybody – good luck and I'll see you on the other side."

No sooner had Hawke finished talking than he had crawled away backwards from the top of the ridge, only standing to his full height when he was sure he was out of sight of the glacier cave's entrance in case anyone was using infrared and was looking for his heat signature. He patted himself down, brushed the snow off and began walking below the ridgeline to the north, where he knew he would be able to track down through the valley.

Showtime.

CHAPTER THIRTY-FIVE

Hawke reached the air vent and broke the grille off with his combat knife. Throwing the metal cover in the snow, he peered down inside the vent and assessed its depth at around thirty metres. Reaching into his pack, he pulled out a length of nylon abseiling rope and after securing it to the steel wall of the air vent, he tossed the other end inside. He unfurled until it was dangling to the bottom of the vent, with some left over. Then he swung his legs inside and began climbing down the rope to the bottom of the vent.

This wasn't the first time Hawke had been able to draw on his expansive training and experience to complete a dangerous task. The duct was a very narrow, confined space and would have made most people feel extremely claustrophobic. Worse than this, if his presence inside the duct was discovered, he was the archetypal 'fish in a barrel', and raking him with machine gun bullets from the bottom of the narrow duct would have been the easiest thing in the world.

He continued down, the cold air from above biting at his face as he descended the nylon rope. The air was being drawn freshly from the environment above, ensuring the inhabitants of the compound had a constant source of clean air to breathe while at work deep inside the ice cave. As he reached the bottom, he saw a blockage in the tunnel – some kind of filter that was in place to remove any impurities from the air coming in from the surface. It looked to Hawke like some kind of HEPA – for a few seconds he was forced to stop and boot it out of the way to allow himself to continue to the bottom of the duct.

He reached the bottom and released the nylon rope, emerging from the duct into a dimly lit room. He scanned his new surroundings and found himself inside what looked like exactly what he had expected. He was standing in some kind of integrated control room where he counted at least four more air conditioning ducts, presumably leading off to various other critical areas in the compound. As far as air quality and temperature were concerned for those deep down inside the compound, this was essentially the nerve centre. As he had discussed above with this team, Hawke now fitted the remote-controlled grenades around the room, ensuring they were out of sight. He would detonate them when the time was right.

He stepped outside of the control room and found himself in a long corridor, the walls lined with advanced thermal insulation tiles, presumably to help maintain a constant warm temperature and insulate the inhabitants from the subzero conditions outside the cave. Moving stealthily, Hawke continued to make his way through the maze-like compound, his MP5 raised into the aim, at the ready. Hearing voices off to his right at a junction up ahead, he slowed his breathing and turned the weapon in the direction of the oncoming people. Two men in white coats walked around the corner in hard hats and holding clipboards. They had no weapons but one of them reached out to smack his palm on an alarm button on the wall to his left. Hawke opened fire and perforated both men, sending them both crashing to the floor in a rapidly expanding pool of blood, thankfully before either of them was able to sound the alarm.

He heard the sound of gunfire echoing through the compound and pulled himself up against the wall to take stock. Looking at his watch, he realised that both teams he had ordered to attack the compound from two different directions outside would by now be in place and engaging with the Director's forces. He silently wished his comrades well and continued to pursue his objective, but only seconds later he encountered more resistance, this time a face he recognised from Eden's briefing on the plane – the man from DC's Cayman Crew known as Dresden.

Dresden recognised Hawke too, although a look of total surprise was on his face now as clearly, this had been the last thing he was ever expecting to see inside the compound. Dresden was armed, both with a combat knife and a pistol secured to a utility belt around his waist. He now reached for the pistol but fumbled the retention flap and gave Hawke all the time he needed to swing his weapon into the aim and release a short burst of rounds into Dresden's chest. The heavyset man from East Germany stared at Hawke with a look on his face suggesting how aggrieved he was that he had failed to draw his weapon in time and do to Hawke what had just been done to him. His blood pressure rapidly dropped and before he was able to say a word he dropped to his knees and then crashed flat on his face, the combat knife and pistol still safely sheathed in their holsters on his utility belt.

Hawke checked the dead man's body for anything of use, particularly a radio or some other way he could hack into the midnight syndicates communications, but found nothing, so continued on his way around the corridor. Reaching a door, he opened it to reveal a lift. Hawke stepped inside and selected the next floor up. The doors slowly closed and the lift began to ascend.

When the lift doors opened, it was to reveal a scale of carnage and chaos that he had very rarely seen before. Outright war seemed to have broken out in what looked like the control room and he only just managed to dive out of the lift and roll for the cover of one of the control panels seconds before DC peppered the lift with rounds in a spirited attempt to take Hawke out of the equation before he had even started. He was startled to see the faces of various world leaders on screens on the far wall. They looked confused and angry, just as he was feeling. Hawke now keyed his comms and tried to locate where the rest of his team was.

"This is Hawke," he said. "I'm calling anyone who can hear me."

"This is Lea. Where the hell are you?"

"I just set the explosives in the control room, so whenever it's time for us to leave this entire place is finished. Where are you?"

"I'm on the other side of the control room. I just saw you jump out of the lift."

"Where's DC?" Hawked asked.

"Ran out of the room. Looks like he might be going up to the next floor," Lea said.

"Where are you, Cairo?" Hawke asked.

"We're on the next floor up, looking for Haggblom," Scarlet said. "I just took out Paris and the one they call Haifa. That means the entire Cayman Crew are out of the game apart from DC himself and Cambridge."

The chatter of gunfire continued relentlessly in the background, and now Hawke felt a burst of rounds chewing into the control panel behind him. He cradled his head instinctively before replying to the others.

"Any sign of Haggblom yet? He asked.

"Not yet," Scarlet said. "But I think he's in an office just ahead of us, at least judging by the amount of security on the door. Unless maybe that's the Director's room?"

"The Director's not down here Lea," said. "I've been looking all over the place for the bastard."

Hawke broke cover and fired on the two men in front of him, cutting them to pieces and killing them instantly. Without wasting a second he sprinted across the control room's upper platform to the position where Lea, Kahlia and Ravi were taking cover, someone chasing him the entire way with an endless fusillade of machine gun bullets always just a few inches behind him. When he finally reached them, he leapt off the upper platform and crashed down beside Lea in a heap of curses and bruised bones.

"I am way too old to be doing this!"

Hawke pulled himself up on the polished concrete floor as the mercenaries at the far end of the corridor continued to hold them in position with a nonstop volley of automatic gunfire. Their rounds ricocheted off the concrete floor and walls, chipping shards of concrete free and filling the air with a fine powder.

"What are you talking about?" Kahlia said. "This is as exciting as it gets."

"You're nearly twenty years younger than me, Kahlia," Hawke said with a grimace. "Think about it."

Another round of gunfire raked over them. Hawke cradled his head in his arms and closed his eyes, waiting for the barrage to come to an end. He was experienced enough in warfare to understand that it would have to come to an end at some point, as the mercenaries reloaded their weapons. That moment had to come because as Hawke had noted, all of them were firing and unloading their magazines at the same time. That also told him something of their professionalism or more to the point the lack of it.

When the firing finally stopped Hawke came back up to the surface, brushing the shards of concrete and powder and dust off his legs, back and shoulders and advancing closer to the mercs, rolling behind the cover of the large steel air conditioning unit. There was no time for further consideration. The men at the far end of the corridor were now moving towards them, randomly sweeping their weapons back and forth to cover every square inch of the control room, if he moved one inch beyond the cover of the air conditioning unit, Hawke knew he would be perforated within an instant.

He took a shot and killed one of the men, then another.

"This is more like it," he said to Lea. "Finally getting back into the swing of things now!"

"I told you it was exciting!" Kahlia said.

"You're both completely insane," Lea said. "Especially you, Josiah! I hope your children are going to be as crazy as you are."

Hawke was slamming a new magazine into his weapon, but now he stopped and looked up at her, confusion growing on his face. "What children?"

"Never mind," she said with her smile widening. "We can talk about that later."

They forged forwards, using interlocking fields of fire to ensure no part of the control room was not covered by their firepower. Ravi threw a grenade taking out another mercenary on the upper level as he tried to climb over a railing and get down to them.

As if communicating telepathically, Hawke and Lea now moved as one, each jumping to their feet and swinging out from behind their cover positions and taking advantage of the men's reloading their weapons to fire several short bursts of bullets into them. Five seconds later, they had cut down nine mercenaries. Then, three other mercs turned tail and ran through a fire door on the right of the room.

"Kahlia! Ravi!" Lea yelled. "Get after them!"

Hawke watched the Hawaiian and the Brazilian take off after the fleeing mercs, leaving just him and Lea to deal with the remaining men in the control room. He had already emptied his magazine and was now reaching into his bag for another. As they advanced across the control room, they took out the remaining mercs and decided to check an office on their left before taking the stairs up to the fight on the next level. It was locked, so Hawke fired his MP5 and blew the lock to pieces, then opened the door and the two of them ran inside. They were both shocked and relieved to see Professor Haggblom sitting in the corner on a wooden chair staring back at them in horror.

"My God! Haggblom said. "I can't believe you finally got here!"

"Yeah... sorry about the delay," Hawke said. "We did have one or two things to do in the meantime. Are you injured?"

"Only my wounded pride," Haggblom said, rising from the chair. "Those maniacs locked me in here while they planned on causing World War Three or something!"

"It's nearly over now," Lea said.

Haggblom looked confused. "How the hell are we going to get out of here?

"Right out through the front door like the honoured VIPs we are," Hawke said. "They've got some jeeps parked up in the front and there's a kind of ice road chiselled out of the glacier that leads to the main cave entrance. Our force has taken out nearly everyone apart from DC, Cambridge and the Witch Doctor... and of course the Director. Scarlet's dealing with them all upstairs as we speak. She thinks their private offices are up there. As soon as they're dealt with we can secure the Crucible and get the hell out of here."

Hawke and Lea turned, poked their head out through the door to ensure there was no one there and then made their way off to their left along the corridor leading away from the control room.

"Why are we going this way?" Haggblom asked.

"These lifts go up to the next floor," Lea said. "As Joe just said, Scarlet tells us that's where the Director's private suite is, so that's where we're gonna find the rest of them. I'd bet my life on it."

Hawke and Lea stepped into the lift and were rapidly followed by Haggblom. As soon as the lift doors closed, Lea pushed the button for the next floor and they readied themselves for another round of fighting. But when the lift door swished open, it was to reveal nothing but silence.

"I wasn't expecting that," Hawke said.

"And I don't suppose you were expecting this either," Haggblom said, burying the muzzle of a handgun into the base of Hawke's skull. He now did the same thing to Lea with a second weapon. "Now, if you wouldn't mind stepping out of the lift, we have some important business to attend to. Move!"

CHAPTER THIRTY-SIX

"Just what the hell is going on?" Lea asked.

"Just keep walking out of the lift," Haggblom said. "I'm touching both of these triggers right now and the slightest move from either of you and you'll both get your heads blown off."

Hawke felt himself tense, but he could feel the gun's cold, steel muzzle pushing into the base of his skull. There was no way he was taking the kind of risk involved in trying to slip away and attack Haggblom from this distance. There was a point-blank certainty he would die.

"Now both of you drop your weapons and we're gonna go for a walk down this nice shiny corridor."

Hawke and Lea both complied and when their guns had clattered to the floor they began walking to the end of the corridor. When they reached the end, Haggblom told them to push through the double doors and they stepped inside a large conference room. There had been a terrible battle in here and the bodies of various people dressed in business suits were heaped all over the floor, gunshot wounds peppering their bodies and bullet marks all over the walls. Hawke guessed this was what was left of the Midnight Syndicate. Sitting around the table was Scarlet, Reaper, Alex, Ravi and Kahlia, the entire team, with their hands on their heads. Standing in the corner, covering them with his machine gun was DC.

"Nice to meet you guys," DC said to Hawke and Lea. "Please join us."

"Yes, take a seat," Haggblom said. "Both of you."

Hawke and Lea obeyed once again, taking a seat beside Scarlet and the others. Lea spoke first.

"Just what the hell is going on, Professor?"

"Questions later," Haggblom said, turning to DC. "Where is the Crucible right now? I have to call the world leaders and tell them about the next phase."

"I sent Cambridge down to get it from the server room with the Witch Doctor. That's what you asked for, Director."

Hawke, Lea and the others exchange shocked glances.

"Wait a minute," Hawke said, are you telling me that you were the Director all along?"

"There's no flies on you," Haggblom said.

Lea looked confused. "Sorry, but I just don't understand what is going on here. We were hired to protect you. Why the hell go through all this? What was the charade for?"

"It's easy enough to understand," Haggblom said. "You'll remember that earlier I told you such was the importance of my work that I was never left unguarded. This was twenty-four hours a day, 365 days a year. What I neglected to tell you was not only was I under permanent guard by these people, but I was also never allowed out of their sight, including anything other than a toilet break. Of course, this was ostensibly to protect me against any kind of threat, but the other reason was to stop me from getting away. There's no trust in government, Agent Donovan. You're talking about senior politicians! At that level, you're talking about a total lack of trust in every direction. From their point of view, I could have decided to slip away and sell my secrets to someone else, retire early and buy a nice private island somewhere."

"You read my mind," Scarlet said under her breath.

"As it is, such a facile and puerile desire would never have crossed my mind. I am after all the inventor of The Crucible."

"The co-creator," Hawke said. "Let's not forget about Professor Marcus Pinkerton."

"Professor Pinkerton had an unfortunate sailing accident this morning on a lake near his vacation cabin in Wisconsin," Haggblom said. "He's no longer part of the equation."

"So, he was never going to be in New York for this meeting?" Alex asked.

"Got it in one!" Haggblom said. "I'm sorry, but the entire thing was a ruse."

"But why?" Kahlia asked.

"Because they're all insane!" Haggblom cried. "All the world leaders are totally, clinically certifiable. Don't tell me you hadn't noticed. As soon as I realised the potential of what the Crucible could do, I grew nervous about handing it over to these maniacs. I know better. The Crucible is the most advanced AI system in the world, decades ahead of all the others, including covert, black ops projects developed by the US, Russian and Chinese militaries. As soon as we solved $P \neq NP$, I knew I was the most powerful man in the world."

"What the hell is that?" Scarlet asked.

"You solved P≠NP?" Alex said, her voice full of shock.

Hawke turned to her. "Is that bad?"

"Would someone tell me what the fuck is going on?" Scarlet said.

Haggblom continued. "P≠NP and P=NP are mathematical, problem-solving equations, in which P stands for Polynomial Time and NP stands for Nondeterministic Polynomial Time. Our world up until my genius a few weeks ago was P≠NP but now it is a P=NP world."

"Is he speaking in English?" Hawke said.

"Yes, sadly," Alex whispered.

"Sadly?" Lea said.

Alex nodded. "Yes, at least as long as he's the only one with this power."

"Put simply," Haggblom said, "a P≠NP world is a world where some problems are easy to verify but hard to fix. A P=NP world, which I have just created, is a world where everything easy to verify is also easy to fix, including the greatest problem for a computer of all, the issue of—"

"Encryption," Alex muttered.

"Encryption!" Haggblom said loudly. "The Crucible has already developed algorithms so efficient that it can instantly break any cryptographic system on Earth. Now you see why…"

"You need a straightjacket," Lea said.

"Why this world needs me," Haggblom said. "I know what this world needs. It needs a new peace. A new settlement. So, I had to orchestrate a kidnapping from the world's best team and that way it would not be questioned. Then I would be free to make this world a better, safer place."

"You're insane," Ravi said.

"Not so," Haggblom said. "As if being able to break any encryption wasn't good enough, it can do so much more. It synthesised a new form of plastic explosive, more powerful than anything in existence in less than an hour. That was the stuff inside your exploding phones if you're interested. Just imagine what else it will do for me!"

"I presume the ridiculous demand made on the billboard was also nothing more than a ruse?" Lea asked.

"Of course!" Haggblom said. "The ransom was made as ridiculous as possible just to keep everybody busy while we inserted the Crucible into the global internet infrastructure."

"So, the Crucible is the source code for a much larger, deadlier AI weapon system?" Alex asked.

"Yes, and very much more," Haggblom said. "And now thanks to Marcus Pinkerton's unfortunate accident, I alone understand how it works."

"But that's not entirely true is it?" DC said out of nowhere.

Haggblom turned on him. "What do you mean?"

"I mean there's someone else who understands it just as well as you – perhaps even better than you."

"If you're talking about the Witch Doctor, then I hardly think so. He is a clever man – a genius some would say – but he was brought onto the project at a very late date. To say he knows more than me would be a wild overstatement."

"Nevertheless," DC said, checking his watch, "he's still been out of our sight for nearly a quarter of an hour now."

Hawke noticed the look on Haggblom's face began to change. "There's not much honour among thieves, is there Haggblom?" he said.

"Where is he now?" Haggblom asked DC.

"I already told you," DC said, his tone changing. I sent Cambridge down with him to get hold of the Crucible when all of this shit kicked off."

"And then what?" Haggblom said nervously. "What are they supposed to do? Did you tell them to rendezvous with you somewhere?"

"Calm down, Haggblom,", DC said.

"Don't tell me to calm down! I haven't given the world leaders their orders yet!"

"That ship has sailed," DC said. "At least for now. Things change, and now we're out of here. You can give your orders another day. In the meantime, I told Cambridge and the Witch Doctor to meet us down by the Jeeps at the end of the ice road leading out to the main entrance. It's all really easy and straightforward. I'll wipe these guys out right now and then the two of us can stroll down there, meet up with Cambridge and the Witch Doctor and get the fuck out of here in one of those Jeeps. We'll be at the airport in less than an hour and before you know it will be airborne."

Haggblom seemed to calm down and now nodded as he silently repeated to himself the plan DC had just outlined. Now he turned to the mercenary and said, "Okay, that sounds good to me. I'll make a head start while you kill everyone in this room and then you come and meet me down on the ice road."

Hawke watched Haggblom shuffle out of the room and then turned his attention to DC, who was slowly strolling towards the same door, but holding a machine gun at the ready. When he reached the door Haggblom had just used to exit the conference room, he turned and raised the gun.

"Talk about shooting fishing a barrel," DC said. "But listen, from one Special Forces guide to all of you, I'm sorry – but it's just my job. Don't take it personally."

He raised the weapon, leaned into the stock and aimed first at Hawke.

CHAPTER THIRTY-SEVEN

Cambridge pulled the wires from the back of the server and dragged them off the shelf. Inside the flat matte-black object, the Crucible was still conscious but trapped inside its digital mind. It was thinking things over, thoughts and calculations that billions of humans over billions of years would never be capable of, finding solutions to problems mankind hadn't even considered yet. Cambridge handed it to the Witch Doctor and the two men scuttled out of the facility, running along the tunnel to the Jeeps.

"I can't believe this is going to work," the Witch Doctor said.

"We're not out yet," Cambridge said. "Haggblom might be stupid enough to let something like this happen, but DC certainly isn't. As soon as he works out he's been double-crossed by us, he'll be right out on our tails until he gets his pound of flesh."

"He can go to hell," the Witch Doctor said, waddling along beside the much fitter man. Under his arm, he gripped the black rectangle containing the Crucible as if he was hanging onto a life jacket and they were running along the deck of a sinking ship.

"Where the hell are we going anyway?" Cambridge snapped, glancing over his shoulder.

"The Jeeps are just up here," the Witch Doctor said, already massively out of breath as they sprinted along the eerie blue ice tunnel. "As soon as we get there, we'll be out of this place in seconds. And then it's just a short drive to the airport. I've already got one of my buddies meeting us there in a helicopter. We'll be at Akureyri Airport in thirty minutes and then Zaugg's private jet is waiting for us. We'll be at her private compound before dawn. DC will never find us, and even if he does, he'll wish he hadn't. Trust me when I say that the kind of people Zaugg has at her disposal makes DC look like a girl guide."

"Let's hope you're right," Cambridge said.

"I am right. And talk of the devil, I've got a call to make."

As they sprinted along the ice tunnel, they turned a gentle bend and saw less than one hundred yards ahead of them four black Jeeps parked up in a row at the side of the tunnel. The eerie blue glow, lit by a string of temporary electric lights banged into the side of the tunnel gave the place an almost haunted feel as their footsteps echoed off the hard ice. With the Crucible still tucked under his arm, the Witch Doctor now took out his telephone and began to hammer in a series of numbers. Desperately out of breath, he was more than a little relieved when he heard the voice of a woman answer his call.

"Hello?"

"Dr Zaugg? This is the Witch Doctor."

"Ah, Mr Kaczmarczyk," Zaugg said. "How good of you to call me. I trust you have good news?"

Ziggy Kaczmarczyk disliked the sobriquet under which he was known throughout the underworld: the Witch Doctor, but everyone called him it. Helga Zaugg was the exception.

"I want all the money you promised me," the Witch Doctor said. "Me and my buddy here don't come cheap and we just put our lives at great risk getting hold of this. The Midnight Syndicate might be massacred, but as far as I know, Haggblom is still alive and so is Franklin Claremont. They will stop at nothing to get this thing back. It's going to be expensive giving me and my buddy the kind of privacy we're going to need to live out our lives in luxurious safety."

"You'll get your money," Zaugg said. "But not until I get the Crucible."

Seconds after Zaugg cut the call, they pulled up at the Jeep to find a woman sitting in the driver's seat. She was just turning the ignition.

"Zarina?" the Witch Doctor said. "What the hell are you doing here?"

"I got away," the Russian woman said. "Care to join me?"

Cambridge and the Witch Doctor looked at each other and shrugged.

"Fine with me," Cambridge said, eyeing her up.

"I'm not so sure," the Witch Doctor said. "She could be spying for Haggblom."

"I hate Haggblom," Zarina said. "I almost killed him myself on many occasions."

Cambridge laughed. The Witch Doctor looked nervously over his shoulder.

"Yeah, sure. I'll take your word for it."

Zarina shrugged. "It's up to you."

Cambridge climbed in beside her. "Let's roll."

The Witch Doctor joined them but didn't look quite so sure as the SAS man now sparking up a cigarette. "If you say so, but Zaugg ain't going to be pleased. She doesn't like changes being made to her plans."

"Don't worry about her, son," Cambridge said and turned to Zarina. "Drive on!"

*

Hawke was fairly certain he was about to meet his maker, but were it not for the fast-thinking actions of Reaper, who now used his substantial bulk to leap from his chair and push the conference table as hard as he possibly could, closing the one-metre gap between the far end of it and DC's legs in less than a fraction of a second.

The American mercenary cried out in pain and made to fire his weapon at the ECHO team who were still trapped down the other end of the conference room, but now Reaper lifted the heavy metal table and using it like a shield, pushed the flat surface of it up hard against DC and crushed him into the wall. From their side of the conference table, they heard DC squeeze off a peel of bullets, which punched through the ceiling tiles above their heads, but by now Scarlet had searched through the bodies of the Midnight Syndicate and found what she was looking for – A Sig Sauer automatic pistol.

She now leaned around the side of the table and shot DC through the head, killing him instantly. He dropped the machine gun and slumped down to the floor. When Reaper slowly pulled the table back down and set it on its legs, DC fell forward and collapsed in a bloody heap on the plush pile carpet.

"Bloody hell! That was good thinking, Reaper," Lea said. "I thought that was the end."

"I couldn't think of anything else to do," Reaper said with his trademark Gallic shrug.

"Neither could I," said Scarlet, "but I know what we have to do now. We have to get down to the ice cave and stop Haggblom, Cambridge and this Witch Doctor guy from escaping. If they get away from here and get to an airport then they could be gone without a trace forever."

Hawke was in full agreement and was already dragging DC's body away from the door which he now flung open and stepped out into the corridor. He reached down and picked up the weapon Haggblom had made him drop moments earlier. After checking it was still loaded, he threw Lea her weapon, and after establishing that Haggblom had rendered the lift inoperable by shooting at the control panel, they turned and made their way back downstairs using an emergency fire escape staircase. When they reached the bottom of the stairs, Hawke booted the door open and the team found themselves standing outside the compound itself, but inside the enormous blue glacier cave.

"You hear that?" Lea asked.

"What do you hear?" Hawke asked.

"Footsteps!" Listen carefully and you can hear footsteps – they're receding, it's Haggblom running away down there!" She pointed to her right, at the narrow passage in between the wall of the blue glacier cave and the polished concrete side of the compound. "He's getting away!"

The team sprinted as fast as they could down the narrow passageway between the glacier wall and the compound before leaving the compound behind them and stepping out into the full width of the ice tunnel. There was a bend up ahead and when they took it they saw Haggblom's silhouette as he sprinted down the ice tunnel in search of his friends.

"Stay where you are, Haggblom!" Lea yelled, aiming her gun at him.

Haggblom ignored her and continued running.

"I said stay where you are or I'll fire on you!"

Scarlet rolled her eyes. "Always by the book."

Haggblom continued to run, and Lea opened fire, punching three shots in between his shoulder blades and felling him like a rotten tree. He crashed down into the hard ice with a sickening smack and then suddenly there was nothing but silence in the tunnel.

"Good shooting," Hawke said. "But we still have to –"

His sentence was broken by the sound of a Jeep's engine firing up.

"Bloody hell! That's Cambridge and the Witch Doctor!" Alex said.

"The bastards must have already got to the Jeeps," Scarlet said. "We have to get after them!"

Hawke began sprinting once again, boots slipping on the blue ice as he made his way at speed around the final bend, and then only to see the red lights of the fleeing Jeep disappearing out of the ice cave's entrance and making a sharp left out into the snowfield.

"We can still catch up to them!" Alex said. "There are three other Jeeps!"

They were still running, and Hawke's dark suspicions about what they might find were confirmed when they reached the Jeeps and saw that Cambridge – a former SAS man, Hawke remembered – had shot holes through all of the tyres and blown the radiators out with bullets.

"None of these vehicles are going anywhere," Hawke said. "We just lost Cambridge, the Witch Doctor and the Crucible."

CHAPTER THIRTY-EIGHT

Helga Zaugg was sitting on the deck of her yacht enjoying an iced vodka when the call came through. She was alerted to the call not by the sound of her phone ringing but by a gentle vibration of her smartphone. She set down her drink, took the phone from her pocket and looked at the screen to check who was calling. She was not surprised. It was the Witch Doctor and his second call to her in less than one hour.

"Why are you calling me again Mr Kaczmarczyk?"

"I'm reporting that we got to Akureyri and we're now safely on board your private jet."

"I've already been told that by the pilot, you fool."

"I'm sorry. I didn't mean to bother you but – "

"Stop talking. You can be of some use to me while you're on the phone," Zaugg said coolly. "Can you confirm that the Crucible is on the plane in one piece and in good working order?"

"Yeah. As far as I can tell, it's in perfect working order," the Witch Doctor said, noting the look on Cambridge's face. The English SAS man was sitting opposite him but one and was already on his second can of lager, his boots up on the seat next to the Witch Doctor. Zarina was in the cockpit talking to the pilots.

"How can you tell?" Zaugg said.

"The physical condition of the Crucible is absolutely fine, at least after a cursory visual inspection. The storage drives look good and so does the cooling system. All of the connectors, cables and external ports are all intact and look to me like they're fully functional. I've already run a diagnostic tool to check for any hardware failures and aside from a small voltage issue everything looks just as good as before."

"Software integrity check?" Zaugg asked. "Mr Grobel here just asked me to ask you."

"I booted the server and I can verify that the operating system is loading up completely correctly without any erratic behaviour. Not only that, the integrity of the Crucible's main AI software itself is totally fine"

"All of this jargon goes right over my head," Zaugg said. "I'll have to take your word for it, Mr Kaczmarczyk.

I'm sure you understand that it's not wise to tell me things that aren't true."

"Everything I've told you is completely true," the Witch Doctor said. "I also ran some checksums and digital signatures and ensured that the software hadn't been meddled with in any way, specifically looking for something to kick in if it was disconnected. None of that is the case. Haggblom had a lot more faith in me than I had in him. I have the full working Crucible right here in my possession."

"Wrong," Zaugg said icily. "I have the full working Crucible right here in my possession – please don't forget yourself, Mr Kaczmarczyk."

"No, I'm sorry," the Witch Doctor said nervously. "When do we land?"

"For me to tell you that would give you some kind of indication as to where you're flying," Zaugg said, "and I'm afraid I can't do that. For the time being, you will have no idea where you are flying, and therefore no idea when you are landing. Both pilots have been briefed to keep you entirely in the dark but fear not Mr Kaczmarczyk, you and Mr Cambridge will be fully enlightened upon landing when you are welcomed to my inner sanctum... just the three of you. You, Cambridge and the Crucible."

The Witch Doctor realised that she had hung up and now, to save face in front of Cambridge, he pretended to say goodbye to her and thanked her for confirming they would be getting the full pay for their work. Then he pretended to switch his phone off and he slipped it in his pocket.

"So, we're getting paid everything she promised us then?" Cambridge asked, downing the rest of his lager and cracking open a third can.

"Yes. She says we're going to get paid in full, but she won't tell us where we're flying."

Cambridge shrugged. "Not the first time I've been on a plane and not known its destination."

"Well, I don't like it," the Witch Doctor said, slowly stroking the fat black square next to him that was the Crucible. "It makes me nervous."

"Just relax, you silly bastard," Cambridge said. "We're home and dry, man. I just read on the news of a vast explosion in northern Iceland. The papers are saying it's something to do with a gas leak but I think we both know it's got more to do with Joe Hawke. He would have taken out the whole damn lot of them, trust me on that. I don't know him but I know men who know him, men from the SBS Regiment years ago. He would have packed that place with explosives before even starting his attack. That means Haggblom, DC... all of them will have gone up in flames. We're safe. No one can get us now."

"Apart from Hawke," the Witch Doctor said.

"Hawke would be completely insane to come after us," Cambridge said. "You're forgetting who we're working for now. Helga Zaugg. As in the daughter of Hugo Zaugg, the man who nearly killed him and his team on their very first mission. No, if old Josiah Hawke's got any common sense, he'll fuck off back to the Caribbean and see his retirement out there, rather than come after us."

"You think that's what he'll do?"

"I don't think it, I know it. He is getting old and he's getting tired and he's been contacting retired members of the Regiment over the last few weeks, talking about packing it in. There's talk of kids with that Irish bird. There's no way he's going to get involved in a massive brawl with Zaugg of all people. Right now, he's getting his sorry arse down to that airport in Iceland and getting ready to go and drink banana cocktails on a tropical beach, which is exactly what I'll be doing when the rest of this fucking nightmare is over. You mark my words, son."

CHAPTER THIRTY-NINE

"Mark my words," Hawke said, "there is no bloody way we are leaving this until every last one of those bastards is tracked down and neutralised. We might have got Haggblom and taken out most of the Cayman Crew, but Cambridge and his little IT Witch Doctor man, are both on the loose. We have no idea where they're going or if they're working for someone else, but we can't discount the idea that they're working for Zaugg."

They were currently sitting inside the Aurora, which was chugging its way back down Skagafjörður, to where Ryan was waiting with Kristjan, They were cold and they were hungry and the cups of hot coffee they had were not doing much to improve their mood.

"That's a bit of a stretch, darling," Scarlet said. "After all, there's just no way we could possibly know such a thing."

"It's Occam's Razor," Hawke said.

"I'd partly agree with that," Ryan said, gently rubbing his leg to alleviate some pain. "The simplest explanation is usually the correct one. On one hand, there are so many psychopaths, nut cases and fruit loops out there that presuming Helga Zaugg is somehow involved with Cambridge and the Witch Doctor is pushing things a bit. But it would be just as easy to make a case that Occam's Razor's 'simplest explanation' is that Zaugg suddenly pops up on our radar and the next thing you know we have the theft of one of the world's most powerful weapons right from under the nose of its creator. I'd say the simplest explanation is that Zaugg is pulling Cambridge and Witch Doctor's strings."

As the boat gently rocked, Alex mulled it over but said she couldn't come to any particular view, claiming it was just too early to make a definitive assessment. Reaper shrugged, finished his coffee and stepped over to one of the portholes, watching the northern lights flickering above the dark black sea beyond.

Lea was sceptical and agreed with Scarlet that it was unlikely Helga Zaugg had anything to do with Cambridge and the Witch Doctor. "I just think it's a bit far-fetched that's all, Joe. I don't think we can attribute every single thing that goes wrong or every single terrorist outrage that happens to Helga Zaugg. We all feel the same way about what her father did, but we have to be careful in painting her with the same brush as him."

"We have to err on the side of caution," Hawke said. "And right now that means not giving Helga Zaugg a sodding inch."

Lea looked at him. "Just take it easy and drink some coffee, Joe. We're all feeling a bit on edge. It's been a long, dangerous night and a long, tough day. We're all tired and we all want to go to sleep. I've already arranged everything with Rich. Richardson's gonna fly us over to Reykjavik and from there, we're getting a jet down to Elysium. We'll wake up in our home. We'll feel refreshed and revitalised then we can go for a walk on the beach and try and put our heads together, try and make sense of what happened here on this mission and what the theft of the Crucible means."

"We know what it means," Hawke said, his voice getting angrier. "It means Helga Zaugg paid Cambridge and the Witch Doctor to steal the Crucible and take it to her. It means she is going to inflict that family's particular brand of depraved evil on the world and now she has the worst weapon on Earth with which to do it. That's what it means."

"Listen, Joe – just do what I said and take it easy. If it is Zaugg then we'll take her down just like we've taken down every single person that's ever crossed us."

"Maybe you're right," Hawke said. "It's just that we're talking about Helga Zaugg and the Crucible – that's one hell of a combination. I just don't see how things can get any worse."

"The only way things can get worse is if we're completely blindsided by something none of us was expecting," Kahlia said. "And that's just not gonna happen because we have a good intelligence network. We know what's going on in the world right now and the only thing on our radar is what you've just described. Cambridge and the Witch Doctor are on the run and the sudden arrival of Helga Zaugg on the scene. That's it."

Hawke nodded, comforted by the coffee and Kahlia's words. "Yeah, I guess you're right. We're tired. I'm exhausted and I'm ready to go to sleep for about twenty-four hours. And I want some decent food and I want to get off this boat. And you're right too, Kahlia. We have to focus our attention on Cambridge and the Witch Doctor and worry about Zaugg later. In the meantime, we pray nothing else comes up."

CHAPTER FORTY

Koru.

It was his name. It meant King in the old language and only kings could bear it. He was a king, King of the Citadel, ruler of the White-Robed Guardians of the Land of the Gods. Sovereign Lord of Kur, the ancient netherworld, the shadowlands, that place that existed parallel to what they called the World of the Others. He was king of it all. No one from the Otherworld knew about this place, but not all their lands were safe.

A man named Faulkner had sent thousands of soldiers to invade the Citadel. He had ordered them to scour the place in search of anything of value whether that be gold, silver, platinum or most likely of all the ancient weapons that his people had protected for countless millennia. Of course, by the time Faulkner's soldiers arrived, there was nothing of value left in the Citadel and the Guardians had moved to another place, a safer place far more out of reach and isolated and rarely visited. The fact that the

Citadel had to be abandoned and forced their retreat to this place, to Kur, was something that both enraged and saddened Koru. He had inherited leadership of his people and assumed responsibility for them and the protection of their most treasured and powerful assets when his father had died, but never in his life or his father's life or his grandfather's life – the two previous kings – had they ever been forced to retreat and hide in this way. Unless they did something to defend themselves, it would only happen again. And this time those from the other world might get their hands on these possessions.

"We have nearly finished building our defences," his son Dugud said.

"It is not nearly enough," Koru said. "We cannot ever allow another force from the Otherworld to breach our defences."

"It will never happen again, Father," Girin said, folding her hands in front of her, her long blonde hair shimmering in the low light. "We are too strong this time."

Koru was not so sure. Their intel operatives worked widely around the world, gathering any data that might be of relevance to their security and well-being. The latest briefings were not encouraging. Helga Zaugg was taking up her father's baton and vowing to continue his work – the work he had inherited from his Nazi Party father – and this meant nothing but trouble for the Guardians.

"You're trying to bring me peace, daughter," Koru said. "You are kind, but there can be no peace until we have driven the likes of Zaugg into the sea."

"That time approaches, father," Dugud said. "A great storm is gathering and it is heading our way."

Koru nodded grimly. "A great storm is gathering, indeed."

THE END

JOE HAWKE RETURNS IN
THE POSEIDON VENDETTA

Author's Note

Here ends another Joe Hawke! Thanks for reading this latest instalment in the series and as always I really hope you enjoyed reading it. I especially enjoyed writing this one, but because I'm not a fan of leaving cliffhangers at the close of books, the twentieth Hawke novel, *The Poseidon Vendetta*, is already written and available for pre-order!

Printed in Great Britain
by Amazon